Arthur Helps

The Life of Pizarro

with some account of his associates in the conquest of Peru

Arthur Helps

The Life of Pizarro
with some account of his associates in the conquest of Peru

ISBN/EAN: 9783337383213

Printed in Europe, USA, Canada, Australia, Japan

Cover: Foto ©Andreas Hilbeck / pixelio.de

More available books at **www.hansebooks.com**

THE LIFE OF PIZARRO,

WITH SOME ACCOUNT OF

HIS ASSOCIATES IN THE CONQUEST

OF PERU.

BY ARTHUR HELPS,

AUTHOR OF THE "SPANISH CONQUEST IN AMERICA,"

"FRIENDS IN COUNCIL,"

ETC.

SECOND EDITION.

LONDON:

BELL AND DALDY, YORK STREET,

COVENT GARDEN.

1869.

PREFACE.

I THINK that some further explanation should be given of the motives which have led to the publication, separately, of the lives of those men who were foremost among the early discoverers and conquerors of the New World, and whose deeds are, for the most part, narrated in " the Spanish Conquest in America." It has been justly asked, Why does the author break up his History in this way? The answer is as follows:—

That History was written with a practical object. The author hoped that the plans which had been adopted by the greatest Spanish states-men for gradually reducing and ultimately obli-terating the evil of slavery, would be of service in the United States. He felt, as every English-man, who knows anything of the subject, must feel, that the British nation, having introduced slavery into its American Colonies, we all were bound to further in any way we could the abolition of that enormous evil. At the time when "The Spanish Conquest in America" was written, there was no immediate prospect of the solution of this great question of slavery by a civil war. In the course of events that History has become, to a certain extent, obsolete. Several persons sug-gested to the author that it would be well to rescue from oblivion certain portions of it. This idea pleased him mainly because he thought that in this way the labours and sufferings of several most notable men in history might be put into a readable form for the world; and amongst them more especially those of one of the most remark-able men in history. He alludes to the labours and sufferings of the " Apostle of the Indies," Las Casas.

In any history of slavery Las Casas must oc-cupy a prominent part. The author of " The Spanish Conquest in America " had been obliged to study the life of that great man with care and minuteness. He thought that it would be an especial pity if his researches into the life of Las Casas should be lost, because the history which embodied them had ceased to apply directly to the present state of the world. The story of the life of·a man like Las Casas is of perennial usefulness. The subjects for the endeavours of great men may change; but the spirit in which these endeavours should be undertaken remains unchanged. There is no man, however great the cause which he advocates, or indeed however small it may be, so that it be one connected with the public welfare, who may not derive something either to instruct, to guide, or to encourage him, in reading the life of Las Casas. I know that it may be said that a biographer is apt to become a blind admirer; but I am sure that the admiration is not in this case misplaced.

The same thing that has been said of Las Casas may be said, in a lower degree, of other heroes who appear in the great tragedy of the Spanish Conquest in America. Columbus, Cortes, Pizarro, Vasco Nunez, were all typical

men. On this account it seemed desirable that
the knowledge which had been gained by an historian respecting these characters—that historian
having written from a peculiar point of view—
should not be altogether lost to the world because
the course of events had happily prevented the
history from being of that service which the author
had intended it to be in practical life, and especially in the national life of our brethren in
America.

INTRODUCTION.

THIS life of Pizarro, like those which have been recently published of Columbus and Las Casas, has been taken mainly from my history of the Spanish Conquest in America.

It has been formed into a biographical narrative by the Rev. F. Watkins, by bringing together the facts about Pizarro, which lay scattered over a long history, and condensing them into a biography.

Amongst discoverers Columbus holds the first place: and Las Casas, Pizarro, and Cortes were also men who may be considered representative men in the several vocations in which they laboured.

Pizarro, for instance, affords the highest type

of a common soldier.   Brave, faithful, enduring, apt in all the exercises and the duties of his calling, he was the very man to form one of a band of invincibles, who would be equally great whether in advance or in retreat, whether as besiegers or besieged—not to be daunted by the extremes of peril or of hardship, nor for a moment neglecting discipline in the midst of unwonted luxury and ease.

There was also something more in Pizarro. Rising from the humblest origin without any education, he is never pretentious; when he comes to command, he is not elated by power; when he gains the highest station, he fills it as if he had been born to it.   He is always calm, polite, dignified.   So much does he bear himself like one who had been born in the purple, that one forgets, and one sees that those around him forgot, that my " Lord Governor " was an utterly ignorant man, who could not even write his own name.   The Spaniards of that age were not a people who by any means undervalued noble birth or learning; but they had also a keen appreciation of what constitutes greatness in a man, and could obey and even reverence one who was neither an *hidalgo*, nor had the slightest pretence to culture.

There were, however, two causes affecting Spaniards (not peculiar to that generation only) which greatly conduced to such a result. The first is, that every Spaniard, whatever may be his birth, is somewhat of a gentleman, and is not ashamed of his position in life, whatever that position may be. It always seems as if he was too proud to wish to be anything else than he is, much more, to put on the appearance of being anything else. Hence he is never vulgar, for all vulgarity may be described as an endeavour to appear to be something different from what we are.

The second cause is this,—namely, that though there are great differences in the various dialects spoken in Spain, there is not one dialect for the higher classes and another for the lower; and therefore a Spaniard may be very poorly educated, and yet speak a language which will not in any way affront the ears of his more refined fellow-country-man. This was, and is, a signal advantage for men like Pizarro, as, when they attain to high station, their language is not necessarily unbecoming that station. That this statement is true as regards the present case, is manifest from the fact that the historians and biographers of the period of the Conquest, when quoting the words of Pizarro, and of others like him, whose rise in life had been very great, never comment upon the language used by these brave men as being low, vulgar, or misplaced.

Pizarro was one of those persons, who, if his lot had been cast in a settled State, and in unadventurous times, would never have risen to any conspicuous position. Whether as a soldier, a merchant, a lawyer, or an agriculturist, he would have been a good, steady, faithful *lieutenant,* but would have been out of place except as second in command.

Placed, however, in such situations as he occupied in the New World—being one in a small band of adventurous men, surrounded by tens of thousands of enemies—passing through countries untraversed before by any European, and having daily to encounter everything that could be imagined that was new and hostile—the humble good qualities which he possessed in such a remarkable degree, the qualities of faithfulness, resoluteness, endurance, and dogged courage, naturally carried him up to the high rank which he has ever occupied as one of the foremost conquerors of the New World.

An exemplary humanity, a keen solicitude for the conquered people, any care for the preservation of works of art and ancient buildings, or wondrous skill in policy, were things not to be expected from a man of his nature and breeding. If he had been taught them, no man would have carried them more resolutely into action. Had he been, for instance, a disciple of Las Casas, he might have been the second in command among the hosts of the philanthropists; but as it was, he has left a name, not without just and high renown, but upon which there are sad stains of cruelty and rapine.

He perished permaturely, as many people do fall in this life, more on account of his good qualities than of his errors and his faults. He was remarkably clement, as clement as Julius Cæsar—that is to his own countrymen. He was singularly unsuspicious—that is, as regards those fellow-countrymen. The first man to suspect an ambuscade of Indians, or any stratagem of warfare he was the last man to believe in the existence of any conspiracy of his fellow-countrymen against himself—against one who, as he knew, was always anxious to maintain their power and increase their welfare.

The favour, too, which he showed his brothers, who were men of the highest ability, and of culture very superior to his own, was a touching proof of the modesty and humility of his character. He knew that they were very superior to him, except, indeed, in the gifts of prudence and moderation, and he was inclined to give them the weight in government which he thought belonged to them rather than to himself.

Conspiracies are mostly very dramatic things; but there is not any conspiracy more dramatic than that which led to the death of Pizarro. From the first you feel, even when ignorant of the result, that a man so confiding as Pizarro was, so confident in the goodness of his cause, merely because it was good, is meant to be a victim. There are few scenes in history more touching than that which took place in the interview between Pizarro and Juan de Rada, the chief of the conspirators; and never do Pizarro's best qualities—namely, clemency, candour, truthfulness, and reliance upon justice, shine forth more conspicuously than in that interview.

After all, it must be acknowledged that Pizarro was not one of the least admirable of those men who have earned a great, though sorrowful renown, from having taken a leading part in the Spanish Conquest in America.

In judging the part such men as Pizarro played in these events we must not forget the stern character of the times they lived in, and their complete and necessary dependence, in their isolation, upon their own firmness and determination. In fact, their training and surrounding circumstances all tended towards the development of severity and tyranny, that is as regards the conquered people; and we can hardly wonder that so few of them have come forth with a fame that after-ages can thoroughly venerate or love.

CONTENTS.

BOOK THE FIRST.

Chapter IV.

Chapter V.

Chapter VI.

BOOK THE SECOND.

Chapter I.

Chapter II.

Chapter III.

Chapter IV.

Chapter V.

Chapter VI.

BOOK THE THIRD.

CHAPTER I.

CHAPTER II.

CHAPTER III.

CHAPTER IV.

Chapter V.

Chapter VI.

Chapter VII.

LIFE OF FRANCISCO PIZARRO.

BOOK THE FIRST.

CHAPTER I.

Francisco Pizarro — His Parentage and Education — His Youth — The first Mention of him in History.

FRANCISCO PIZARRO, the discoverer and conqueror of Peru, was the natural son of Gonzalo Pizarro, an officer who greatly distinguished himself in the Italian Wars under the " Great Captain,"* and who was of an ancient and wealthy family of Truxillo, in the province of Estremadura.   Francisco's mother was also of a noble family of Truxillo; her name was Francisca Gonzales.

Francisco Pizarro had four brothers—Fernando,

---

* Gonzalo, Fernandez, de Cordoba.

Gonzalo, Juan, and Martin.   Of these Fernando alone was legitimate. They all seem to have been in possession of some landed property in Spain; for when they joined their brother Francisco to assist him in his conquest of Peru, it is said that Juan, Gonzalo, and Martin sold their estates. Francisco, however, does not seem to have been so well off; for his sword and his cloak were the only possessions with which he set forth to seek his fortune in the New World.

There is a great deal of uncertainty as to the date of Francisco Pizarro's birth; but according to Quintana, Gomara, and other historians, he was born at Truxillo, in the year 1470. The information attending his birth being so vague it is not remarkable that we find many fables respecting it; one of them to the effect that he was left by his parents on the steps of a church, where he was found being nourished by a sow.

We know very little concerning his early years, except that his education appears to have been totally neglected, as he could neither read nor write, and, from what we can gather as to the youth of this embryo discoverer, some part of his childhood was passed in fulfilling the ignoble office of a swineherd. There is little doubt that he served, as a mere lad, with his father in the Italian wars. Even in his younger days, when placed in subordinate positions, he was never heard of as a rebellious or contentious man; but on the contrary, as I gather, showed himself to be laborious, cautious, obedient, much-enduring and faithful. Whatever he did and accomplished was done by his own dogged perseverance, and when once he had undertaken an enterprize, he would go through with it, whatever the consequences.

When the prize which he had for years set his mind upon seemed about to be grasped by others, he quietly withdrew, until their too impetuous eagerness had ruined them; and then stepped forward to carry out what they had failed in. It was most unfortunate, indeed, for the world that this perseverance of his was so great; for, had the conquest of Peru been postponed but a few years, it would probably have met with a more consolidated state of affairs in that kingdom, and, therefore, ultimately, have been a more effective conquest.

We then have nothing to relate concerning

him of any importance till the year 1510, when Ojeda (one of Columbus's followers in his second voyage to the Terra Firma) having obtained the government of the province of Urabá and founded the town of San Sebastian, left Francisco Pizarro there in the command of his forces, as lieutenant, under circumstances of no ordinary kind.

At this time Francisco Pizarro was forty years old. What he had gone through since his arrival in the New World may be best gathered by considering what is known of Ojeda, his commander; for the circumstances in which Ojeda left him at San Sebastian were such as to prove that it would have been the height of madness and thoughtlessness in any commander to have deserted his men, unless he knew he was leaving them under the care of some well-known, well-tried, and trustworthy lieutenant.

My readers will see that, in this life of Pizarro, much matter has been introduced concerning the commanders and discoverers with whom, and under whom he served. This has been found to be absolutely necessary, for the life of Pizarro is so inseparably connected with that of such men as Ojeda, Pedrarias, and Vasco Nunez, that it was impossible fully and faithfully to relate his deeds, without including in my narrative much that relates to those men with whom he was so closely associated, and a great portion of whose lives and adventures was so entwined with his, that, if omitted, this biography would have been but a bald and incomplete picture of Pizarro's undertakings and surroundings.

Columbus, Cortez, and Vasco Nunez were from the first leaders in the great expeditions and discoveries which are connected with their names; whereas Pizarro, rising from the ranks, performed a part well-deserving of commemoration in expeditions and discoveries which are not ordinarily associated with his name.

CHAPTER II.

*Ojeda—His treacherous Capture of Caonabó—Obtains the
Government of Urabá—Joins with Nicuesa—Founds San
Sebastian—Is in great difficulties—Leaves Pizarro there
as his Lieutenant—Loses his Power—Dies a Monk.*

THIS Ojeda had sailed with Columbus
on his second voyage from Spain to
the New World. His personal strength
was immense. Placing himself at the bottom of
the Giralda, at Seville, he could throw an orange
to the top, a height of two hundred and fifty feet.
In early life, in the presence of Queen Isabella,
he had walked out and back on a plank stretched
out from the top of the Giralda. Indeed, Columbus chose him out of all his men to perform a
deed requiring no small amount of daring, resolution, and unscrupulousness. The admiral, upon
his second arrival at Hispaniola, found a cacique
—Caonabó, who in former days had put to death

the garrison at La Navidad—preparing to attack that of St. Thomas; and, indeed, but for his opportune arrival, threatening to sweep away the whole of the Spanish settlements in the island. A battle was fought, and the Spaniards were victorious. A horrible carnage ensued upon the flight of the Indians; but Caonabó, being absent from the battle, besieging the fortress of St. Thomas, remained untaken. The admiral resolved to secure his person by treachery.

The story,* which was current in the colonies, of the manner in which Ojeda captured the resolute Indian chief, is this: Ojeda carried with him gyves and manacles, the latter of the kind called by the Spaniards, somewhat satirically, *esposas* (wives), and all made of brass (laton) or steel, finely wrought and highly polished. The metals of Spain were prized by the Indians in the same way, that the gold of the Indies was by the Spaniards. Moreover, among the Indians there was a strange rumour of talking brass, that

---

* The learned Muños considers this story as a legend. (See the prologue to his history). I do not know why it should be so considered.

arose from their listening to the church-bell at Isabella, which, summoning the Spaniards to mass, was thought by the simple Indians to converse with them. Indeed, the natives of Hispaniola held the Spanish metals in such estimation, that they applied to them an Indian word, *Turey*, which seems to have signified " anything that descends from heaven." When, therefore, Ojeda brought these ornaments to Caonabó, and told him they were Biscayan *Turey*, and that they were a great present from the admiral, and he would show them how to put them on; and that Caonabó should set himself on Ojeda's horse, and be shown to his admiring subjects, as, Ojeda said, the kings of Spain were wont to show themselves to theirs, the incautious Indian is said to have fallen entirely into the trap. Going with Ojeda, accompanied by only a small escort, to a river a short distance from his main encampment, Caonabó, after performing ablutions, suffered the crafty young Spaniard to put " the heaven descended " fetters on him, and to set him upon the horse. Ojeda himself got up behind the Indian prince, and then—whirling a few times round, like a pigeon before it takes its determined flight, making the followers of Caonabó imagine that this was but display, they all the while keeping at a respectful distance from the horse, an animal they much dreaded—Ojeda darted off, and, after great fatigues, now keeping to the main track, now traversing the woods in order to evade pursuit, brought Caonabó bound into the presence of Columbus. This, however, took place sixteen years before the time when Ojeda left Francisco Pizarro as his lieutenant to stave off, as best he could, the war, pestilence, and famine, that were more than decimating his men at San Sebastian.

Columbus, in his first two voyages, had only discovered the islands in front of the mainland of America. But in his third voyage, in the year 1498, he reached the mainland, and touched at Paria. Ojeda probably was with him; for the next year, having been aided by a knowledge of the admiral's route, he accomplished a somewhat similar voyage on his own account, having on board that personage, who makes a dubious figure in the history of the New World—Amerigo Vespucci, and a very celebrated pilot of that time, called Juan de la Cosa. Another voyage was made about the same time to these parts by Rodrigo de Bastidas, with the same Juan de la Cosa for pilot; and this was remarkable for the presence of the renowned Vasco Nuñez; and the knowledge this man gained there had the greatest influence on the fortunes of his varied and eventful life, and indirectly on that of Francisco Pizarro. During all this time, Francisco Pizarro —nobody thinking much of him—was doing the work of a second-rate soldier in a stern, creditable manner.

Ojeda, soon after this, favoured by Bishop Fonseca,* obtained the appointment to the government of the province of Urabá, and took with him Francisco Pizarro, as his lieutenant. A man, of good birth, a good speaker, and a good musician, of the name of Nicuesa, obtained the adjacent government of Veragua. The two governments comprised the whole of the Isthmus of Darien, and a large extent of country to the east and north-west. Ojeda was poor, but he was aided in furnishing his expedition by the cele-

---

* Bishop of Burgos, and afterwards President of the Council for the Indies.

brated pilot, Juan de la Cosa, and by a lawyer, named Martin Fernandez d'Enciso. Ojeda sailed for his province, and, entering the port of Carthagena, began to make war upon the Indians. He marched upon a large Indian town, called Turbaco, which he found deserted. He pursued the fugitive Indians, and, while doing so, his men spread themselves over the country in a disorderly manner. The Indians, seeing this disorder, collected together, and came down suddenly upon the Spaniards, who, in their turn, had to become the fugitives, and to take refuge in a fort constructed hastily of palisades. The Indians gave the Spaniards no rest, and, having poisoned arrows, pressed the advantage they had gained with so much vigour, that they succeeded in putting all the Spaniards to death, to the number of seventy or a hundred, with the exception of Ojeda and one other.

His fleet, ignorant of what had befallen their chief, was quietly coasting along. At last, however, gaining intelligence of what had happened, his men went to seek him, and found him almost speechless with hunger, his sword in his hand, and the marks, it is said, of three hundred arrows in his shield. They made a fire, warmed, and fed him. As he recovered, and while he was relating his adventures to the men, Nicuesa's fleet hove in sight. The contest between these two governors, while they were at St. Domingo, having been carried on in the most offensive and personal manner, Ojeda might well expect ill-treatment from Nicuesa, or at least contempt; but Nicuesa was angry at anybody imagining that he could take advantage of his present superiority to punish former affronts, and assured the men he would be a brother to Ojeda, and, upon his being produced, received him most kindly.

The two governors then joined company, and went with four hundred men to seek for Juan de la Cosa, and to chastize the Indians. No quarter was given. They fell upon Turbaco, committed incredible slaughter, burning the Indians in their cottages, and slaying men, women, and children. Then, having discovered the body of Juan de la Cosa, who had been killed by poisoned arrows, they returned to their ships.

Ojeda now took leave of Nicuesa, and made his way to the Gulf of Urabá. Entering the Gulf, he endeavoured to find the river Darien, which the two governors had agreed to accept as the boundary of their respective territories. This river he could not discover, but he disembarked on the eastern side of the gulf, and founded a town on a height there, calling it San Sebastian.

Ojeda sent his stolen gold and Indians home to Saint Domingo, in order that more men and supplies might in return be despatched to him; and he inaugurated the building of his new town by a foray into the territories of a neighbouring Indian chief, who was reported to possess. much gold. This foray, however, produced nothing for Ojeda, and his men were soon driven back by clouds of poisonous arrows.

How their people should be fed seems always to have been a secondary consideration with these maurauding governors. It appears as if they supposed gold to be meat, drink, and clothing,—the knowledge of what it is in civilized and settled communities perhaps creating a fixed idea of its universal power, of which they were not able to divest themselves. Famine now began to make itself felt at San Sebastian; but fortunately at this time, there came in sight a vessel which had been stolen from some Genoese; for it was thought that the new settlement would be a place, where the title to any possessions would not be too curiously looked into. The supplies, which this vessel brought, were purchased by Ojeda, and served to relieve for the moment his famishing colony. But their necessities soon recommenced, and, with their necessities, their murmurings. The Indians also harassed them by perpetual attacks, for the fame of Ojeda's deeds was rife in the land. The Spanish commander did what he could to soothe his people, by telling them that Enciso, the partner in his expedition, and his alcade, was coming. And as for the Indians, he repelled their attacks with his usual intrepidity. These, however, began to understand the character of the man they had to deal with, and, resolving to play upon his personal bravery, laid an ambuscade for him, in which he was shot through the thigh with a poisoned arrow. He ordered two plates of iron, brought to a white heat, to be tied on to the thigh, threatening the reluctant surgeon to hang him, if he did not apply this remedy. It was so severe, that it not only burnt up the leg and the thigh, but the heat penetrated his whole body, so that it became necessary to expend a pipe of vinegar in moistening the bandages, which were afterwards applied.

The supplies brought by the stolen vessel being now entirely consumed, Ojeda's company began to feel again the pressure of famine, and to murmur accordingly. They also took counsel among themselves about seizing furtively the brigantines and returning to Hispaniola, for they disbelieved, or affected to disbelieve that Enciso was coming at all. Ojeda resolved to anticipate their designs, and in these straits, to return himself to Hispaniola. He did so; and it was under these circumstances, and in command of his discontented and famishing men, that Francisco Pizarro was left as lieutenant.

Ojeda reached Saint Domingo after innumerable sufferings and difficulties, but never regained power and influence. He lived for some time afterwards at St. Domingo, and died in extreme poverty. It appears that he became a Franciscan monk for a few hours before his death, and was clad in the habit of that order when he died, " making," as Oviedo assures us, " a more laudable end than other captains in those parts have done."

CHAPTER III.

Pizarro in the Neighbourhood of the Pacific—Takes his men away from San Sebastian—Meets Enciso, Ojeda's Partner —Vasco Nunez—The Expedition returns to San Sebastian —Nicuesa—Nicuesa turned adrift—Vasco Nunez takes the Command.

FRANCISCO PIZARRO was thus left in command on the Terra-firma, with only a narrow isthmus between him and his destiny; for within a few days' journey, flowed the Pacific, and on its coast Peru with all its riches—that country with which his name was so soon to be associated for ever.

Still, the fixed idea, which is to take possession of him and haunt him night and day, alluring him onward like some phantom, had not yet entered his mind. He is the soldier of fortune—patient, laborious, much-enduring—but no more.

He has proved himself to be anxious, never

resting, never much excited, never desponding, cautious, reserved, taciturn, willing to do his best for the benefit of all, submitting to obloquy, patient of murmuring and discontent among those, who are under him. In those qualities he is superior to the men, among whom he lives; but the idea, which is to kindle him into enthusiasm, and to flash out into something like genius, is yet to come. And, but for a very remarkable coincidence, that idea would perhaps never have come, and Francisco Pizarro would have lived and died, without raising his head above the mass of men; and Peru would have had some other name joined with it, as its conqueror, and no doubt for the better; at least, it could hardly have been for the worse.

When the fifty days had expired, for which Pizarro and his men were to wait for Ojeda's return, and there were no signs of their commander, it was resolved to dispeople the settlement and to sail away. But, as the two brigantines would not hold them all, they were obliged to wait, until hunger and the assaults of the Indians had reduced them to the proper number. Then they killed and salted the horses that were left, and, having thus provided themselves with some food for the voyage, they embarked; Pizarro commanding one of the brigantines, and a man, named Valenzuela, the other. Their sojourn at San Sebastian had lasted six months.

When they were twenty leagues from the shore, Valenzuela's brigantine, struck, as it was imagined, by some large fish, went down suddenly. Pizarro made for the port of Carthagena, and, as he entered, saw a ship and a brigantine coming in at the same time. These proved to contain the men and the supplies, brought at last by the Bachiller Enciso, Ojeda's alcalde mayor. He had with him one hundred and fifty men, several horses, arms, powder, and provisions. But that was not all; the most important part of the cargo is yet to be mentioned. In the midst of the cargo, unknown to its owner, was a barrel, containing no provisions, but a living man, who was destined to have the greatest influence upon Pizarro's future life. His name was Vasco Nuñez de Balboa, a native of Xeres de Badajoz, an adventurer, a skilful master of the art of fencing (*digladiator*); who, as he was in debt, and, as indebted people might not leave the island of

Hispaniola without the permission of the authorities, had secretly, by the aid of a friend named Bartolomé Hurtado, contrived to get into this barrel, and to form part of Enciso's stores. When the vessel had got out to sea, Vasco Nuñez made his appearance, much to the dissatisfaction of Enciso, a precise lawyer, who must thoroughly have objected to aid in any breach of the law. He threatened to put Vasco Nuñez on a desert island, but suffered himself to be pacified at last. To those who know the part, that Vasco Nuñez was about to play, it almost seems as if the Arabian story of the unfortunate man, who freed a malignant spirit from durance, and found that it had sworn to destroy the person, who should deliver it, was so far about to be acted again.

On the meeting of the remnant of Ojeda's company under Pizarro's command with the reinforcements brought by the Bachiller Enciso, the latter commander at once concluded that these people had fled away from their duty, and had deserted Ojeda. Indeed, Enciso was so convinced of this, that he was inclined to put them into confinement, and at first would give no credit to the story they told him. Their famished appearance, however, was an undeniable witness in their favour, and at last they succeeded in convincing the Bachiller of the truth of what they were saying; and then, naturally enough, they did all they could, Pizarro no doubt joining with them, and, from his position, having more weight than any, to dissuade him from proceeding to San Sebastian; but he, full of his lawyer-like notions that he must do what he had contracted to do (and he is to be honoured for this), resolved to go on to Urabá; and, partly persuading them with a hope of plunder, partly insisting upon their obedience, he contrived to carry them along with him.

Thus was Francisco Pizarro again carried back towards the scene of his destiny; and that it was decidedly against his better judgment may be gathered from the state of despondency, into which they were thrown after their arrival at San Sebastian.

Just as Enciso was making for land near San Sebastian, from some oversight on the part of the man at the helm, his vessel was thrown upon a rock, and in a very short time beaten to pieces. The men with difficulty saved themselves in the boat and the brigantine, but all the cattle and almost all the provisions were lost; and, when Enciso and his men made their way to San Sebastian, they found the fortress entirely destroyed. Their situation was manifestly most perilous. For some time they managed to subsist upon wild animals caught in the mountains, and upon the buds of the palm tree; but this precarious supply soon came to an end, and then it was necessary to obtain food by force.

The Indians here, however, as Ojeda had found before, were most formidable opponents. It is mentioned that three naked Indians with poisoned arrows pierced as many Spaniards, as they had arrows for, and then fled like the wind.

In these straits we may easily imagine how the desire to return grew upon the men, and how Pizarro and the remnant of Ojeda's people clamoured at their advice and entreaties not having been listened to. And now, while Pizarro was wishing to turn his back on the Pacific, as yet unknown, and the nations lying on its coast,— while the hearts of all men in this colony were thus stricken down, Vasco Nuñez spoke out. He said that he recollected, when he was with

Rodrigo de Bastidas, entering this gulf of Urabá; and that they disembarked on the western part of it, where they found an Indian town near a great river, in the midst of a fertile country. He also said, which was most to the present purpose, that the Indians in those parts did not use poisoned arrows. How deeply it is to be regretted that this knowledge of poisoned arrows did not overspread the continent; for, as every reader of the Iliad is always on the Trojan side, so it is impossible, in reading of the conquest of the New World, not to wish for the success of the weaker party, or, at least, not to regret that their weapons were for the most part so lamentably unequal to those of their invaders.

This river, that Vasco Nuñez spoke of, proved to be the river Darien. His advice was instantly listened to; and the Bachiller Enciso, taking with him Vasco Nuñez and a hundred men, set out to find the Indian town. They succeeded in finding it; but the Indians, who had heard of their doings in other parts, were not inclined to receive them amicably. Five hundred men (the women and children having been sent away) had taken up a position on a hill, awaiting the orders of Cemaco, their cacique, for battle.

Enciso's forces were victorious, for Vasco Nuñez proved to be right in his report of there being no poison in the arrows of these Indians; who accordingly made no resistance, worthy of the name, to the blows of sword and lance dealt by the Spaniards.

Enciso afterwards entered the Indian town, where he found a store of provisions; and, pursuing his researches, he discovered in a cane-brake the household gods of the Indians, among which were also found golden breastplates and golden chains. Sending for the rest of his people from San Sebastian, Enciso founded the town of Santa Maria de la Antigua del Darien.

But these Spaniards under Enciso, the partner of Ojeda, were to the north-west of the river Darien, and consequently in the government of Nicuesa: it is necessary, therefore, to inquire what had become of him in the mean time. Indeed, no sooner had Enciso's men a season of relief from their immediate sufferings, than, disappointed and discontented, they used this very ground, as a pretext for getting rid of their commander—namely, that they were no longer in Ojeda's territory, but in that of Nicuesa; which

was true.   Vasco Nuñez was, no doubt, at the
head of the malcontents.   The men, resolving to
depose Enciso, proceeded to an election of their
officers; and, in straits like these, a good choice
is nearly sure to be made.   They chose Vasco
Nuñez and a man named Zamudio, for their
alcades, and a person of the name of Valdivia,
for regidor; but even this election was not decisive in the minds of these unfortunate colonists.
There still remained three factions, one in favour
of Vasco Nuñez, another devoted to Enciso, and
a third to Nicuesa.

An accident determined the matter in favour
of Nicuesa.   It was always the custom with these
governors, when they went on their expeditions,
to leave behind some one, who should constantly
send men and supplies after them.   Nicuesa had
left behind him in Hispaniola his lieutenant, Rodrigo de Colmenares, who was to take charge of
the stores and provisions, which were to follow
him.   Colmenares met with great hindrance from
the authorities in Hispaniola, and it was not
until ten months, after his chief had sailed, that he
was able to follow him.   The first point he had
touched upon in the Terra-firma was in the pro-

vince of Santa Martha, on Nicuesa's side of the river Darien. From thence he had proceeded westward or north-westward along the coast, in search of Nicuesa, making smoke-signals on the shore and firing off guns, which were at last heard by Enciso's men, who, returning the signals, brought Colmenares to them. This was in November, 1510, when Pizarro was forty years old.

The provisions, which Colmenares brought in his ships, were powerful arguments in favour of Nicuesa; the recollection of his pleasant manners, and of his kindness to their late commander, Ojeda, must have told in his favour; and, in fine, the greater part of Enciso's company joined in sending Colmenares to Nicuesa, to ask him to come and take the command of them. Again are the Pacific and its nations on the point of being thrust out of the grasp of Vasco Nuñez and Pizarro; but fortune decreed it otherwise. Nicuesa had been as unfortunate in his expedition, as Ojeda had been in his; for soon after quitting Carthagena, where he had left Ojeda, as the weather had now become very contrary; one stormy night, to avoid danger near the coast, he put out to sea, and in the course of that night parted company with all the other vessels. In the morning, thinking that his fleet had perished, he returned to the coast and went up a river, of which the name is not given. There the tide, flowing out with a great rapidity unperceived by the ship's crew, left him on a sand-bank. The caravel instantly fell on its side, and began to go to pieces. Nicuesa and his ship's company were only saved by the boldness of one of them, who contrived to fasten a rope to a tree, by which, as on a bridge, the men made their way to land, but all the stores, provisions, and clothes were lost.

One thing, however, of value remained to them,—the boat. In that Nicuesa put four seamen, and ordered them to coast along to the west, keeping near him, while he and the rest pursued their course by land. Thus they proceeded for some days, and on one occasion, imagining they could save much distance by going all of them from one promontory to another, where the land made a great curve inwards, they all used the boat by turns, and got safely to the opposite headland; which headland, however, proved not to be part of the coast, but a desert island, where there was not even fresh water. The four men, who managed the boat, went off with it one night, and Nicuesa and his men were left to endure the extreme of suffering.

His fleet in the meantime, concluding that their commander would be sure to make his way to Veragua, resolved to hold on their course in that direction. When they had all come together in the river Chagre, the second in command, Lope de Olano, finding that there were no tidings of the chief, concluded he was lost, and, by general consent, took the command of the expedition. But it was no longer in a hopeful state. The ships had suffered from a worm, which was very destructive to ship-timber on that coast, and all the provisions had been spoiled or lost. In a short time Lope de Olano finds himself on the shore near the river Belem, with the great ships knocked to pieces and a caravel formed out of them, with his two brigantines, with no stores, no provisions, and many of his men dead. Here he is found by the four mariners, who had stolen away with the boat from Nicuesa and the rest, leaving them on a desert island.

A brigantine was sent to fetch off Nicuesa and his companions; and they rejoined the rest at the river Belem. The first thing Nicuesa did on meeting his people was to command the arrest of Lope de Olano, and bitterly to reproach his other principal officers, for not having made efforts to discover him.

Meanwhile, the state of things around him grew worse and worse, but the severity of Nicuesa's temper did not abate; and his men believed that he absolutely took delight in imposing upon them dreadful burdens, when he sent them into the country to see what they could get by force from the Indian villages. To such an extremity were the Spaniards reduced, that on one occasion they are said to have been driven by hunger to cannibalism.

Nicuesa at length resolved to leave a spot, that had been so fatal to him. Taking with him in the caravel and the two brigantines their complement of men, he left the others behind, and set sail, directing his course to the east.

They put in at a harbour, which proved to be Portobello, so named by Columbus. But they were now so weak, that they could hardly hold

their weapons in their hands. The Indians succeeded in resisting them, and in killing twenty.
From Portobello they went sailing towards the
east, until they came to another harbour. In the
name of God (*en nombre de Dios*) let us stay here,
they exclaimed; and Nombre de Dios is the name
the port has ever since retained.* What poetry
and history there are in names! Here Nicuesa
sent for the rest of the men from the river Belem.
Since his departure from Belem he had lost two
hundred more men; and now, of the seven hundred and eighty-five men, who came out with him
from Hispaniola, there remained in December,
1510, only about a hundred. Hunger, which
had dogged the steps of this expedition from the
night of that fatal tempest and dispersion, still
relentlessly pursued them. At last, all the ordinary rules of discipline were at an end, and there
could not even be found one man in the company strong enough to do the duty of a sentinel.

It was just at this moment of extreme and
apparently hopeless peril that Colmenares, pur-

---

* It afterwards became the great fort for the reception
and transmission to Spain of the riches of Peru.

suing steadily his course westward, came upon their track and found them. Great was the delight of the seventy men who remained,—for their number had now dwindled to seventy; and Nicuesa's delight was not the least, when, shedding tears, he threw himself at the feet of one, who brought him present safety and such good hopes for the future. Indeed, it was a change of fortune such as seldom occurs, except in fiction.

According to Peter Martyr's account, Colmenares found Nicuesa "of all living men the most unfortunate, in a manner dried up with extreme hunger, filthy, and horrible to behold;" and now he was summoned to become governor to those, who remained of his rival Ojeda's force, and who, unfortunate as they had been, had at any rate made a less wretched settlement than Nicuesa and his men could boast of having done.

But Nicuesa's good temper and good sense were not now to be recovered by any gleam of good fortune. Hearing that Ojeda's company had collected gold, upon which, since, strictly speaking, they were settled in the country assigned to him, he had some claim, he gave out that he should take it away. The disgust, which the deputies from Darien began at once to conceive for him, may be easily imagined; nor was this disgust likely to be diminished by any good words, that would be said of him by his own men at Nombre de Dios. Lope de Olano, though in chains, contrived to put in his word, privately telling the new comers that Nicuesa would do with them, as he had done with his own people, when they sent for him from the desert island. Lope de Olano's words had the more effect, as he was able to communicate with some relations and men from his own province, Biscayans, who were at Darien. Still, had Nicuesa been swift in acting upon his good news, he might have anticipated the consequences of his foolish and tyrannical sayings, and have defeated his Biscayan enemies; but, while he sent on to Darien a caravel, in which there were many of the people, who murmured against him, he himself in the brigantine stopped on the way for about a week, to reconnoitre some little islands and to capture Indians, for which iniquity there came a terrible retribution. No sooner had the people in the caravel reached Darien, than they began to influence the colonists there against him, and with such success, that the

Darienites became quite mad with themselves at their folly, in having invited Nicuesa. It may easily be imagined, and was generally reported that Vasco Nuñez did what he could to incite the people against the coming governor; and it is said that he canvassed with great secresy the principal persons, man by man, convincing them of their error in having chosen Nicuesa, and showing them the remedy for it.

When, therefore, Nicuesa neared the place of disembarkation, expecting to be received with whatever pomp men so tattered and buffeted could show, he found an array of armed men drawn up on the shore, looking as if they meant to repel an invasion, rather than to receive a governor. The procurador, in a formal manner, proclaimed aloud that Nicuesa should not be permitted to land, but return to his own settlement at Nombre de Dios.

The next day, when he appeared, they called him to them, meaning to take him prisoner; but, being remarkably swift of foot, he escaped them. He then asked them to take him for a companion, if not for a governor; and if not as a companion, as a prisoner; saying they might put him in chains. But they only mocked him. Vasco Nuñez, who had some grandeur of soul, did his best to make them change their behaviour; and he .even inflicted the punishment of a hundred stripes on one of those, who took most part against Nicuesa; but, seeing that he could not resist the whole settlement, he sent privately to Nicuesa, telling him not to trust himself among them, unless he could see him, Vasco Nuñez, with them. Nicuesa gave no heed to this, for, afterwards, when there came a deputation to him in mockery, he listened to them, and placed himself in their hands. But no sooner had they got him into their power, than they made him swear that he would go away, and not stop, until he should appear before the King of Spain and his Council. In vain the wretched Nicuesa protested against their cruelty in sending him away so ill-provisioned as he was for any voyage. They paid no attention to his entreaties, but turned him adrift in the most wretched brigantine that was there. And so Nicuesa set sail from Darien, and was never heard of more.

Thus is another man removed, under whose guidance this expedition would either have miserably perished, or confined itself to paltry descents upon the Indians, or to the establishing of unimportant settlements on the northern coast of Darien, while, on the southern, the Pacific and nations, rich beyond all conception, were only waiting to be discovered. Of the companions, whom Ojeda and Nicuesa brought out with them full of hope and proud designs, only forty-three remained of Nicuesa's men, and thirty or forty of Ojeda's. The rest of the men, now at Darien, were those, who had come in the reinforcements brought by Enciso to Ojeda, and by Colmenares to Nicuesa. Pizarro, as the trusted lieutenant of Ojeda, was now of no small weight among the men; but it was as a subordinate rather than a chief. The man, who rises to the surface as chief, is Vasco Nuñez de Balboa.

CHAPTER IV.

Vasco Nuñez takes the command—Sends away Enciso—The Expedition is nearly failing—The Cacique Careta—Vasco Nuñez loves his daughter—The Cacique Comogre—Comogre's son — The young man's speech — Tidings of the Pacific and rich nations southwards — Pizarro listens eagerly—The return to Darien—Messengers are sent to the Court of Spain—Enciso's enmity to Vasco Nuñez—Rumour of a Governor for Darien—Vasco Nuñez determines to discover the Pacific—First sight of it—Pizarro sent to discover the shortest way to the coast—Pearl-fishing — Tidings of the riches of Peru—They return to Darien— A messenger is sent to the Court of Spain.

IT is interesting to notice the way in which great deeds, which are waiting to be done, refuse, as it were, to be done by the men set in authority to do them, and, falling through their hands, remain to be done by men, who, when these deeds were first taken in hand, were in but a subordinate position, and altogether precluded from taking any prominent part with reference to them.

When Nicuesa and Ojeda first set out for their respective governments on the Isthmus, Vasco Nuñez remained behind at Hispaniola in such straitened circumstances, that he was forbidden to leave the island. Francisco Pizarro was employed in the expedition, but any fame or gain that might have accrued to it would not have fallen to his lot; he was no more than one out of many of the officers serving under Ojeda; and yet these two men, Vasco Nuñez and Pizarro, were the very men, who were to accomplish all that was destined to be done. It was little dreamed that the conduct of that enterprise was to devolve upon a man, who should furtively come out in a cask to evade his creditors. By the time of Ojeda's removal from the scene, Vasco Nuñez had so worked himself into the affections of the men, that a very considerable party chose him for their commander, in opposition to Nicuesa and Ojeda's partner, Enciso. It is remarkable that at this juncture Pizarro, though looked upon as a good captain, is not thought of as a chief, a proof that the grand idea of his life had not taken possession of him—

that as yet he was a man of no purpose, capable of serving, but unable to originate and lead. It was fortunate, therefore, for Pizarro's future fortunes that the command of the expedition was not allowed to remain in the hands of such men, as Ojeda and Nicuesa.

This Vasco Nuñez had most of the qualities necessary for a commander in those times. He was forward in enterprise, far-seeing, fertile in resources, crafty, courageous, goodhumoured, and handsome. I think, too, he had considerable nobility of nature; and I am not disposed to lay the whole blame of the treatment, which Nicuesa received at the hands of his men, upon Vasco Nuñez. His conduct to Enciso is far more questionable, and has justly laid him open to the accusation of having kept in mind the threats and reproaches Enciso addressed to him, when he made his unwelcome and undignified appearance from amidst the cargo of Enciso's vessel.

After Nicuesa's departure, Vasco Nuñez instituted a process against the Bachiller, saying that he had usurped a jurisdiction, to which he had no claim, as he had not received authority from the King, but only from Ojeda, who was already

dead.   Upon this poor pretext, Vasco Nuñez
sequestered Enciso's goods, and put him in prison, but afterwards freed him upon the understanding that he should sail for Castille or for
Hispaniola.   It seems a very weak proceeding
of Vasco Nuñez to have sent home a man, who,
he must have known, would be a powerful enemy;
but he took care to send in the same ship Valdivia and Zamudio,—Valdivia to go to Don Diego
Columbus at Hispaniola, and Zamudio to go on
to Spain, and there represent to the King the
services, which the colonists at Darien had rendered to his Highness.   Valdivia did not go
empty-handed.

Vasco Nuñez, having heard that there was
much gold in Cueva, a province at thirty leagues
distance, sent Pizarro with six companions to
discover this province.   The Indians in this part
did not use poisoned arrows; Pizarro, therefore,
was able with that handful of men to beat back,
and kill great numbers of the natives, before returning to Vasco Nuñez.   Another incursion was
made into these regions; but the Indians had
now learned to take refuge in flight.   There are
signs now of Vasco Nuñez getting discouraged

with the enterprise; and here was the turning
point of his career; if he had been a man like
Ojeda or Nicuesa, he would have contented himself with making petty incursions, have thus
deprived himself of the neighbourhood of the
Indians, and eventually have perished from star-
vation. After some little time, as Nicuesa did
not return to Darien, of which event it appears
Vasco Nuñez had an expectation, he sent for the
remnant of Nicuesa's men from Nombre de Dios.
As these people were on their way to Darien,
and were in a port of the province of Cueva, there
came to meet them two Spaniards, without clothes,
and with painted bodies, like the Indians. These
were men, who, about a year and a half before,
had fled from Nicuesa's ships to avoid punishment, and had been kindly received by Careta,
the cacique of Cueva. Indeed he had made one
of them, Juan Alonzo, his chief captain. This
wretch bade the Spaniards tell Vasco Nuñez
that, if he would come to Careta's town, he would
deliver his master, the cacique, bound, into the
hands of Vasco Nuñez; and he also gave the
alluring intelligence that there were great riches
in that province.

Vasco Nuñez was delighted at this news, and came immediately into Careta's territory at the head of a hundred and thirty men. He captured Careta, carried him and his family to Darien, and devastated the town. The cacique, however, was not on this occasion ill-treated by the Spaniards; but, on the contrary, was conciliated and converted into a most useful ally. He gave his daughter to Vasco Nuñez, who loved her much; and the cacique entered into an agreement (here we may trace the wisdom of the Spanish commander) to aid in growing supplies for the Spaniards, if they would assist him in carrying on war against his enemy, Poncha.

This is the way, in which an invading force generally makes its footing good in a country,—by converting the foolish enmities of the natives into stepping-stones of conquest. The above conditions were agreed upon and fulfilled.

Forty leagues from Darien, and adjoining Careta's territory, was a country called Comogra, situated on the sea-coast, the cacique of which country was named Comogre. This chief was brought into friendship with the Spaniards by one of Careta's relations, and Vasco Nuñez went to visit him. The Spaniards were much surprised by the signs of comfort and civilization, which th.y found in this Indian chief's dwelling; the chief himself gave them a splendid welcome, and presented them with four thousand *pesos* of gold and seventy slaves. While the Spaniards were weighing out this gold, there arose, to use the expressive words of an old translation of Peter Martyr, a " brabbling among the Spaniards about the dividing of the gold."

Comogre's eldest son, seeing this miserable contention among the Spaniards, was disgusted at their clamour. So, after the fashion of Brennus, dashing with his hand the scales, in which the gold was, and scattering it about, he made the following speech, " What is this, Christians; is it for such a little thing that you quarrel?* If you have such a love of gold, that to obtain it you disquiet and harass the peaceful nations of these lands, and, suffering such labours, banish your-

---

* Peter Martyr adds, " —— and that you make so much turmoil about a little gold, which nevertheless you melt down from beautifully wrought work into rude bars (for they carried their melting instruments with them)."— Dec. ii. cap. 3.

selves from your own lands, I will show you a country, where you may fulfil your desires. But it is necessary for this that you should be more in number than you now are; for you would have to fight your way with great kings, and among them, in the first place, with King Tuba-namá, who abounds with this gold, and whose country is distant from our country six suns."

Then he signified to them that this rich terri-tory lay towards a sea, and southwards; at which sea they would arrive, he said, after passing over certain sierras. It was navigated, he added, by ships with sails and oars, a little less in size than those of the Spaniards. Traversing that sea, they would find a land of great riches, where the people had large vessels of gold, out of which they ate and drank; where, indeed, there was more gold than there was iron in Biscay—(it appears that the shrewd Indian had been making inquiry with respect to the manufacture of the Spanish swords). The above is not to be taken as a speech set down in a classical history, but it appears that the substance of it was really uttered by the young Indian prince. Juan Alonzo and the other Spaniard, who had lived with King

Careta, served as interpreters; and these men seem to have been fated to be the conduits, as it were, of great evil, and their intelligence the cause of great adventures.

It appears, moreover, that the young prince informed his attentive audience that a thousand men would be requisite for this undertaking; and that, when asked for the grounds of his information, and for his advice, he made another speech, in which he told the Spaniards that his countrymen, too, had wars, and that he had learned these facts from one of his own men, ("Behold him!" he exclaimed,) who had been a captive in those countries of which he spoke. He also offered to accompany the Spaniards; and he said that they might hang him on the next tree, if his words should not prove true. The substance of his speeches, and probably some of the exact words were conveyed to the Spanish Court. This was the first notice of the Pacific, and also of Peru. It is likely that Pizarro was a bystander. Much, however, yet stood between him and Peru. If the expedition were to discover Peru the day following, it would be but little to him,—a few *pesos* more of gold and silver, a few hundreds of slaves; but to Vasco

Nuñez would belong all the principal glory and benefit. He, Pizarro, was a painstaking, trust-worthy captain, but no more. But there is no doubt that among all those captains, who, as Peter Martyr says, " marvelled at the oration of the naked young man, and pondered in their minds, and earnestly considered his sayings," there was none, upon whom this oration had a deeper and more lasting effect.

The Spaniards, having baptized Comogre and his family, giving him the name of Don Carlos, took their leave and returned to Darien, joyful and thoughtful, in the feverish state of mind of persons seeing before them great enterprises, for which they are not quite prepared. When they arrived, they found that Valdivia had come with a ship and some provisions, also with a gracious message from the authorities of Hispaniola; but their provisions were consumed in a few days, and famine, always dogging their steps, soon began to attack them again. It was not alto-gether their own fault this time, for a great storm had destroyed what they had sown. They lived now, as some of the feudal barons in the middle ages did, by predatory forays, robbing and de-vastating wherever they could.

Vasco Nuñez has been held to be a man, who dealt very wisely, and, upon the whole, very mercifully with the Indians; but we are told that he was accustomed to put them to the torture, in order to make them discover those towns, which had most gold and provisions, and then to attack these towns by night. He wrote to the admiral, saying that he had hanged thirty caciques and must hang as many as he could take; for the Spaniards, being few, had no other course, until he should be supplied with more men. He meant that terror was his only means of supplying the defect of force.

Still the resistance of the Indians continued. Conspiracy after conspiracy against the Spaniards was formed among the caciques, but by one means or another the conspiracies were broken up or frustrated; and at last, by the treachery of a native woman, Vasco Nuñez was able to direct his captain, Colmenares, to the spot where the forces of the caciques were assembled; and Colmenares, falling suddenly on Tirichi, captured the confederates, seized their provisions, put the chiefs to death, and terrified the whole country into submission.

Vasco Nuñez and the colonists at Darien now resolved that a messenger should be sent to the

King of Spain, to inform his Highness of what had happened, to tell him of the speech of Comogre's son, and to seek for countenance and succour. Vasco Nuñez wished to go himself, thinking probably that he could plead his own cause best at court; but his companions would not hear of this,—a proof that it was felt how the welfare and existence of the whole colony depended upon him. They chose Quicedo and Colmenares as their deputies, who were well furnished with funds for their important mission; but their means of transport were of the most miserable description. With a very scanty stock of provisions, and with not a soul on board, who knew anything of navigation, in a crazy vessel, the deputies from Darien left that colony in October, 1512. As was to be expected, they made a very bad passage; and, being driven to Cuba, and afterwards going to Hispaniola, which was in accordance with their instructions, they did not arrive in Spain until May, 1513.

One part of their intelligence seems particularly to have caught the fancy of their countrymen at home. An Indian had mentioned that there was a river, where the natives fished for gold with nets; the deputies repeated this story; and as all persons, from the weakest to the strongest, thought that this was a kind of fishing, at which they would be singularly expert and fortunate, all Spain became anxious to fish in those waters.

Unfortunately for Vasco Nuñez, the deputies from Darien were not the only persons of that colony at this time present at the Court of Spain. The Bachiller Enciso was there too, and no doubt loud and bitter in making his complaints of Vasco Nuñez. Besides, there was the intelligence of what had happened to Nicuesa; and as it appeared that Vasco Nuñez had been the greatest gainer from Nicuesa's repulse, he had also to bear the greatest part of the blame for that transaction. The king ordered him to be proceeded against criminally; and in the civil courts he was cast in all the expenses, to which Enciso had by his means been put.

Meanwhile Vasco Nuñez had no easy time at Darien, where factiousness reigned supreme. It appears that there was a man named Hurtado, whom Vasco Nuñez favoured much, and to whom he entrusted much authority. This man became particularly obnoxious to several of his comrades.

These, uniting, sought to take prisoners both
Hurtado and his chief; but Vasco Nuñez, who
was always alert, made the first move, seizing
the head of the opposing faction, and putting him
in prison.   He was afterwards released, and the
dispute for the moment suppressed.   Many of the
men on the last division of gold had accused their
commander of unfairness; and, as there was a sum
of ten thousand *castellanos* just about to be divided, they determined to make this the pretext
of seizing upon his person.   The way, in which
he surmounted this difficulty, may serve to show
the abilities of the man for command.   Far from
seeking to be the great personage in this important
business, on the very evening of the day of par-
tition, or the day before, the politic Vasco Nuñez
went out to hunt, and left his enemies to seize
upon the gold, and divide it.   They, as was to be
expected, made enemies in doing so, and loosened
the bands of their own faction; while those, who
were injured, or who thought they were, made a
great tumult, recalled Vasco Nuñez to full power,
and put his enemies in prison.

About this time there arrived at Darien two
vessels with a hundred and fifty men in them,

laden with provisions, which had been sent from Hispaniola by the Spanish authorities in that island. These ships also brought something, which was very welcome to Vasco Nuñez, namely, his appointment as captain-general.

This was done by the treasurer at St. Domingo. Any show of authority was very welcome to Vasco Nuñez; and, in his joy, as if it had been a birth-day, he willingly consented to let loose all the prisoners, as an act of grace, upon the receipt of good news.

However, amidst all these flowers of rejoicing there came some adder-like news, which must have filled the heart of Vasco Nuñez with apprehension; and that was the report of his own dis-favour at court, caused by the complaints of the Bachiller Enciso,* and by the intelligence of Ni-cuesa's fate. I should think that the rumour of the king's intention to appoint a governor of

---

* The error of Vasco Nuñez in his treatment of Enciso followed him throughout his career. But indeed this is a common case in ordinary life, as a large part of the best time in many men's lives is spent in extricating themselves from the consequences (or in enduring them) of one or two thoughtless blunders.

Darien was very likely to have accompanied this news, which came in a letter from Zamudio, a former colleague of Vasco Nuñez.

His position was most perilous. The maxim, *confugiendum est ad imperium*, must have occurred to him, not exactly in the words of the original, for Vasco Nuñez had little learning, but only by that intuitive knowledge, which great peril, coming upon great resources of mind, easily strikes out. In truth, it is melancholy to observe, as wise men have done, how much of private misery is at the bottom of great actions, and what sleepless furies have driven many an Orestes to enterprises, that were transcendently difficult, but not so difficult as staying still, or so painful as looking backwards.

Vasco Nuñez therefore resolved to be the discoverer of that sea and of those rich lands, to which Comogre's son had pointed, when, after rebuking the Spaniards for their brabbling about the division of the gold, he turned his face towards the south. In the peril, which so closely impended over Vasco Nuñez, there was no use in waiting for reinforcements from Spain; when these reinforcements should come, his dismissal would come too. Accordingly, early in September, 1513, he out set on his renowned expedition for finding "the other sea," accompanied by a hundred and ninety men, well armed, and by dogs, which were of more avail than men, and by Indian slaves to carry the burthens. He went by sea to the territory of his father-in-law, King Careta, by whom he was well received, and, accompanied by whose Indians, he moved on into Poncha's territory. This chief took flight, as he had done before; but Vasco Nuñez, whose first thought in his present undertaking was discovery not conquest, sent messengers to Poncha, promising not to injure him. The Indian chief listened to these overtures, and gave Vasco Nuñez guides and porters from among his people, and enabled him to prosecute his journey.

Following Poncha's guides, Vasco Nuñez and his men commenced the ascent of the mountains, until he entered the country of an Indian chief, called Quaregua, whom they found fully prepared to resist them. The king and his principal men were slain, and a total rout of the Indians ensued.

Leaving several of his men, who were ill, or over-weary, in Quaregua's chief town, and taking with him guides from this country, the Spanish commander pursued his way up the most lofty sierras, until, on the 25th of September, 1513, he came near to the top of a mountain, from whence the South Sea was visible. The distance from Poncha's chief town to this point was forty leagues, reckoned then six days' journey; but Vasco Nuñez and his men took twenty-five days to accomplish it, as they suffered much from the roughness of the ways and from the want of provisions.

A little before Vasco Nuñez reached the height, Quaregua's Indians informed him of his near approach to the sea. It was a sight, in beholding which for the first time any man would wish to be alone. Vasco Nuñez bade his men sit down; while he ascended, and then, in solitude, looked down upon the vast Pacific—the first man of the Old World, so far as we know, who had done so. Falling on his knees, he gave thanks to God for the favour shown to him, in his being permitted to discover the " Sea of the South." Then with his hand he beckoned to his men to come up. When they had come, both he and they knelt down and poured forth their thanks to God. He then addressed them in these words: "You see here, Gentlemen and Children mine, how our desires are being accomplished, and the end of our labours. Of that we ought to be certain; for, as it has turned out true what King Comogre's son told of this sea to us, who never thought to see it, so I hold for certain that what he told us of there being incomparable treasures in it will be fulfilled. God and his blessed Mother, who have assisted us, so that we should arrive here and behold this sea, will favour us, so that we may enjoy all that there is in it."

Afterwards, they all devoutly sang the " Te Deum laudamus;" and a list was drawn up by a notary of those, who were present at this discovery, which was made upon Saint Martin's day.

Every great and original action has a prospective greatness, not alone from the thoughts of the man who achieves it, but from the various aspects and high thoughts, which the same action will continue to present and call up in the minds of others, to the end, it may be, of all time. And so a remarkable event may go on acquiring more and more significance. In this case, our knowledge that the Pacific, which Vasco Nuñez then beheld, occupies more than one half of the earth's surface, is an element of thought, which in our minds lightens up, and gives an awe to this first gaze of his upon those mighty waters. To him the scene might not at that moment have suggested much more than it would have done to a mere conqueror: indeed, Peter Martyr likens Vasco Nuñez to Hannibal, showing Italy to his soldiers.

Having thus addressed his men, Vasco Nuñez proceeded to take formal possession, on behalf of the kings of Castille, of the sea and all that was in it; and, in order to make memorials of the event, he cut down trees, formed crosses, and heaped up stones. He also inscribed the names of the monarchs of Castille upon great trees in the vicinity.

Descending the sierras, he entered the territory of an Indian chief, called Chiapes. The Indians were disposed to make a valorous resistance, but were soon put to flight. Vasco Nuñez sent messengers to Chiapes with overtures of peace, which were accepted. Quaregua's Indians were now sent back home with presents;—conduct, which was very politic; for it conciliated and re-assured the Indians thus sent back; it gave confidence to the fresh ones who accompanied him; and it prevented him from being overburdened with Indians, who might rather impede than advance the march. In truth, throughout this expedition Vasco Nuñez seems to have acted with great sagacity.

While he was in the town belonging to Chiapes, he sent on Francisco Pizarro, Alonzo Martin, and others, to find the shortest way to the sea-shore. Alonzo Martin was the first to discover it. He then descended to the shore, and found two canoes, lying high and dry in a place, where he could perceive no sea. At this he was astonished; but, the sea making its appearance, and gradually advancing to the canoes, he entered one of them, begging his companions to bear witness that he was the first to float upon that sea. Pizarro and Alonzo Martin returning with their intelligence, Vasco Nuñez himself went down to the shore, accompanied by eighty of his men. He entered the sea up to his thighs, having his sword on, and with his shield in his hand: then he called the bystanders to witness how he touched with his person and took possession of this sea for the kings of Castille, and declared that he would defend the possession of it against all comers.

His energy was inexhaustible; and, " not being able to be quiet, even while his bread was being baked," he resolved to navigate a certain gulf in those parts, to which he gave the name of San Miguel; a name it still retains He made his way to the country of a chief, named Tumaco, in a corner of the gulf. With some little difficulty he conciliated this chief, who sent for ornaments of gold, and two hundred and forty large pearls, which he presented to the Spaniards. He also desired his people to fish for more. The Spaniards could hardly contain their joy. One thing alone occurred to damp it. The Indians, not knowing better, were accustomed to open oysters by means of fire; this injured the colour of the pearl; and, accordingly, the Spaniards diligently taught the Indians the art of opening oysters without fire,— with far more diligence, indeed, than they expended in teaching their new friends any point of Christian doctrine.

It was said that this cacique, Tumaco, spoke of the riches of Peru to Vasco Nuñez; and there is something to countenance this in the report of the Spanish commander's letter to the king; for he says, that he had learnt from Tumaco wonderful secrets of the riches of that land, which for the present he wished to keep to himself.

Vasco Nuñez, after having given some attention to pearl-fishing, resolved to return home to Darien, but by a different route from that, which he had taken in coming. He learnt that, to get to Darien by this route, he would have to pass through Tubanamá's country. This was the much-dreaded chieftain, of whom Comogre's son had made mention in his speech. Vasco Nuñez made a forced march upon him, came upon his town suddenly by night, and captured him and his family. He, however, released him, ordering him to collect gold and send it to him, and, pursuing his course, came to Comogra. The labours and changes of climate he had endured began to tell even upon the hardy Nuñez; for we hear that he suffered now from fever, and was carried in a litter borne by Indians. The old chief, Comogre, was dead; but the eldest son, who had made that eloquent but unwise speech, the cause of so much mischief, was reigning in his stead. By him Vasco Nuñez was hospitably entertained; and doubtless they had many things to hear from, and to tell each other. In a few days, having recovered from the fever, he pursued his way to Darien. As if to crown his good fortune, when he entered Poncha's territory, he found messengers from Darien to tell him that two ships, well laden with provisions, had arrived from Hispaniola. Taking a chosen body of his men as an escort, he hastened onwards, and on the 29th of January, 1514, reached Darien; which he had quitted on the 1st of September, 1513; this most important expedition having occupied not quite four months.

His men at Darien received him with exultation; and he lost no time in sending his news— "such signal and new news"—to the king of Spain, accompanying it with rich presents. His letter, which gave a detailed account of his journey, and which, for its length, was compared by Peter Martyr to the celebrated letter, that came to the Senate from Tiberius, contained in every page thanks to God that he had escaped from such great dangers and labours. Both the letter and the presents were entrusted to a man named Arbolanche, who departed from Darien about the beginning of March, 1514.

In his letter to the king, Vasco Nuñez mentioned that he had not lost a man in these battles with the Indians.   But, indeed, why should he have done so, for what was there in their simple weapons and innocent mode of warfare, that could, unless by accident, destroy a well-armed man?

CHAPTER V.

Pedrarias appointed Governor of Darien—His character— The eagerness of men to come out with him—The return of Enciso—The old colonists deliberate how they shall receive the Governor—Vasco Nuñez recommends a welcome recep- tion—Vasco Nuñez's audiencia—He is put into confine- ment, but afterwards released—Darien unhealthy—Seven hundred of the new colonists die—Pedrarias begins to send out expeditions—Pizarro leaves Vasco Nuñez's faction— Goes out with Gaspar de Morales as second in command— The cruelties committed—All these expeditions unsuccessful —The melting-house shut up—Reflections.

VASCO NUÑEZ had now established himself, and might have been considered as destined by Fortune to be the dis- coveror and conqueror of Peru: Pizarro is still comparatively unknown, little thought of, undis- tinguished from the ordinary run of subordinate captains; and little likely to carry out anything, that Vasco Nuñez might fail in. It is probable, too, that in the eyes of Vasco Nuñez, who, like all great men, was undoubtedly a good judge of men and their abilities, Hurtado and Colmenares both possess more genius and fitness for command than Pizarro; but it is not always that genius and striking abilities carry the day; perseverance often succeeds where they fail. Pizarro, it is probable, spoke little, but reflected much. His quiet steady perseverance is undoubted; and that, in time, when the opportunity came, stood him in the stead of genius, and accomplished very astonishing results. Fortune now at this time made a great move in his favour.

The rumour, which had reached Vasco Nuñez, and had made him undertake at any risk the enterprise in search of the Pacific, in which he had been so successful, was not a false one: the Spanish government had appointed, even before he began that enterprise, a governor for Darien. It is probable that previously even to the arrival of Quicedo and Colmenares, who had been sent by Vasco Nuñez with an account of what Comogre's son had told him, the appointment of the governor was quite settled.* The news, brought

---

* They arrived in Spain in May, 1513, and the date of Pedrarias's appointment is July 27, 1513

by these deputies from Darien, served to heighten the importance of the appointment, and greatly to augment the numbers of the expedition.   As all Spain was in a state of excitement at the idea of fishing up gold with nets, the appointment of Governor of Darien was much sought after; but ultimately was conferred upon the man, whom the Bishop of Burgos (who afterwards was President of the Council for the Indies) favoured, namely, Pedrarias de Avila.

He was an elderly man of rank, of high connections, of much repute in war, having served with honour in Africa; but in wisdom he does not seem to have been superior to Bobadilla.* From his feats in the tournament he had acquired the name of " Justador," the jouster.

----

* " I often imagine him (Bobadilla) to have been such a man as may often be met with, who, from his narrowness of mind and distinctness of prejudice, is supposed to be high-principled and direct in his dealings, and whose untried reputation has great favour with many people; until, placed in power some day, he shows that to rule well requires other things than one-sidedness in the ruling person; and is fortunate, if he does not acquire that part of renown, which consists in notoriety, by committing some colossal blunder, henceforth historical from its largeness."—Helps's *Sp. Cong.*, i. 170.

There is one thing to be said for the appointment of men of that age and station, which, if it occurred to King Ferdinand, would have been very likely to have had great weight with him. It is that they are nearly sure of being faithful to their sovereign. It is too late to form great independent schemes of their own; but then they lack the lissomness of mind, as well as of body, which is necessary in dealing with such entirely new circumstances, as those which the Spanish captains in the New World had to encounter. I conjecture Pedrarias to have been a suspicious, fiery, arbitrary old man. " Furor Domini " was a name given him by the monks in after days; just as Attila enjoyed and merited the awful title of the " Scourge of God."

Comogre's son had said that a thousand men would be necessary to make their way to the sea, and to obtain the riches, which were there to be obtained. For greater safety twelve hundred was the number assigned to Pedrarias for his armament, and fifteen hundred was the number which went; for it happened that there was a great disbanding of troops at that time, and the men thus set free were anxious to enter the service of Pedrarias.

When Pedrarias arrived at Seville, he found no fewer than two thousand young men eager to be enrolled in his forces, and " not a small number of avaricious old men," many of whom offered to go at their own expense. It was necessary, however, not to overload the ships; and, therefore, many of these candidates were rejected. Among those chosen were several nobles. A bishop also was appointed to the new colony, whose name was Juan de Quevedo.

Gonsalvo Hernandez de Oviedo, the celebrated historian, went out as veedor in this expedition, Gasper de Espinosa as alcalde mayor, and as alguazil mayor the Bachiller Enciso, whose appointment boded no good to Vasco Nuñez. It must be borne in mind that Enciso had been the partner of Ojeda, Pizarro's former commander, and so may probably have had some influence in detaching Pizarro from Vasco Nuñez.

Pedrarias set sail with his men from the port of San Lucar in twelve or fifteen vessels, on the 12th of April, 1514. Vasco Nuñez's messenger, Arbolanche, reached the Court of Spain too late by far for his master's interests, for he only departed from Darien in the beginning of March, 1514.

This expedition under Pedrarias was one of the greatest sent out to the Indies in those times, and it cost the King of Spain a very large outlay. Had it been under the command of a wise and great man like Columbus, or even of a great commander like Cortes or Vasco Nuñez, it might have been the beginning of a wise colonization of South America. But great means seldom come into great hands, or perhaps the world would advance too fast; while, on the contrary, the most important and successful experiments are often made, like those of renowned inventors in mechanics or chemistry, with few, shabby, and ill-fitting materials.

On the voyage Pedrarias had an opportunity of manifesting the severity of his character, as, for a comparatively slight act of disobedience, he caused one of his own attendants to be hanged, and thus created terror throughout the fleet.

Before reaching Darien the armament entered the harbour of Santa Martha, and thence, pursuing its course westward, touched at the Isle Fuerte, and afterwards, entering the Gulf of Urabá, made its way to the new settlement of Santa Maria de la Antigua del Darien.

Immediately on the arrival of the fleet in the Gulf of Urabá, Pedrarias sent a messenger to Vasco Nuñez to inform him of his arrival. The messenger did not find Vasco Nuñez surrounded by any of the usual signs of power and splendour, but clothed in a cotton shirt, loose drawers and sandals, overlooking and helping some Indians to put a straw-thatch on a house. On hearing the message, Vasco Nuñez, who had no doubt well considered his part, sent a respectful welcome to the new governor, and said that the colonists were ready to receive him. The little colony now consisted of four hundred and fifty soldiers, men inured to danger, and, to use the expressive words of the original, " tanned with labours." It is said that there was much discussion among them as to how they should receive Pedrarias; and the historian Herrera thinks, but not justly as it seems to me, that these four hundred and fifty men could have mastered the fifteen hundred whom Pedrarias brought with him. In a month's time this might have been so; but at present these fifteen hundred men, being chosen persons, full of hope and confidence, admirably equipped, and with the terror of the king's name, would have scattered Vasco

Nuñez's men like chaff before the wind. Counsels of peace prevailed; and it was agreed that they should go out unarmed, and in the peaceful dress of magistrates, not of soldiers. The old colonists, therefore,—one of them certainly with a heavy heart, but all with apparent joyfulness— came out to meet their countrymen, singing the *Te Deum.* Pedrarias landed and billeted his men. This was on the 30th of June, 1514.

It is a custom, I believe, even in our own times, that, in some departments, the minister coming in should have a long conference with the minister going out; and if this is requisite in settled countries, it was far more so in those new-found states, where the inhabitants, the climate, the provisions, the geography, and the mode of warfare were all unknown to the new comers. On the day after his arrival, Pedrarias summoned Vasco Nuñez to his presence, and with gracious words respecting the appreciation of Vasco's services, which was now entertained at Court, requested him to give an exact account of this new land, and of the men who inhabited it. Vasco Nuñez replied fittingly to this courtesy, and promised to give an account in writing, which he did in the course of two days, and which contained the whole narrative of his administration, that had now continued for three years. He also described the rivers, fissures (*quebradas*), and mountains where he had found gold, the caciques whom he had made allies (these were more than twenty), and his journey of discovery to the South Sea and to the " Rich Isle," as it was called, of pearls. It is probable that Vasco Nuñez may on this occasion have given some account of what he supposed to be the population of Darien, which is stated to have been above two millions.

The first thing after this to be done was to take the *residencia* of Vasco Nuñez, the result of which was that, for the injuries done to Enciso and others, he was condemned to pay several thousand *castellanos*, and was put into confinement, but afterwards, in consideration of his services, was set free.

The next thing was to make settlements in those territories, where Vasco Nuñez had suggested they should be made, when he was advising the expedition to discover the South Sea. But in the mean time Pedrarias's people began to fall ill. The situation of Darien was very unhealthy ; and the new comers not only suffered from the effects of the climate, but from those of sheer hunger. On disembarking, the provisions brought by the fleet had been divided among the men, but the flour and the greatest part of the provisions were found to have been spoilt by the sea. The old colonists were not in any way prepared for such an accession to their numbers, and there were no neighbouring Indians who might assist in such an emergency. The expedition had thus sailed into the very jaws of famine. Men clad in silks and bro-cades absolutely perished of hunger, and might be seen feeding like cattle upon herbage. One of the principal hidalgos went through the streets saying that he was perishing of hunger, and in sight of the whole town dropped down dead. In less than a month seven hundred men perished.

Pedrarias himself was taken ill, and by the advice of physicians went to a station at a little distance from the town. All these misfortunes delayed the sending out of the expeditions, and probably indisposed the minds of men for the adventure they had come upon.* They must

---

* Some of the principal men were allowed to return to Spain; and they went to Cuba, and many engaged in the expeditions sent out from that island.

have felt disappointed and desperate, and therefore were ready for any cruelty.

One of the first of his captains, whom Pedrarias
sent out, was Juan de Ayora, who entered into
the territories of Vasco Nuñez's friendly chiefs,
to make settlements there. He proved himself a
terrible tyrant, and undid all the good, that Vasco
Nuñez's wise policy had begun. He obtained
a large quantity of gold, but neither the king,
nor Pedrarias, nor the expedition was any the
better for this gold, as Juan took ship, and, furtively making off with his plunder, was never
heard of more in Darien.

There are signs, however, of an understanding
springing up between the governor and Vasco
Nuñez; for the bishop, who had come out with
Pedrarias, suggested that Hurtado, the great
friend and ally of Vasco Nuñez, should be sent
out to see " what God had done with the lieutenant Juan de Ayora."

The next enterprise worth mentioning is that
entrusted to the Bachiller Enciso, but it was
attended with no results. It is probable that all
this time the prudent and thoughtful Pizarro had
never once forgotten what he had heard of the

nations of the South Sea; for he holds himself aloof from every expedition, that is not directed to those parts.

But now Pedrarias determines to send one under Gaspar de Morales to the South Sea, to find pearls in the islands in the Gulf of San Miguel. Vasco Nuñez had been anxious to visit these islands, but had been dissuaded from doing so by his friend Chiapes. Pizarro joined himself to this expedition, and was employed as second in command. It committed the most dreadful cruelties, and aroused the most deadly hatred in the Indians.

They formed a great conspiracy to destroy Morales, in which no fewer than twenty caciques were concerned. By torture Morales managed to obtain some intelligence of what was going on, and succeeded in defeating the plans of the conspirators. The caciques, whom he captured, he gave to his dogs to tear in pieces. And yet in this very territory Morales had been received in the most friendly manner. He now directed his course to the territory of a cacique, called Birú, at the eastern end of the Gulf of San Miguel. It is conjectured to have been from a corruption of his name that the great kingdom of Peru was so called. This chief pressed the Spaniards so closely, that, though victorious, they did not think it worth their while to stay in his territory. Morales made, therefore, his way, with all speed, back to Darien. Meanwhile, the people of the caciques, whom he had thrown to his dogs, joined themselves to the Cacique Birú, and hovered about his rear. To free himself, the Spanish commander, had recourse to a most cruel expedient. He stabbed his Indian captives at intervals, as he went along, hoping thus to occupy the pursuing Indians. This incident is alluded to in becoming terms of indignation by Vasco Nuñez, now a critical observer of other men's doings, in a letter to the king, where he says that a more cruel deed was never heard of among Moors, Christians, or any other people. Oviedo speaks of this transaction as an " Herodian cruelty," and states that ninety or a hundred persons perished through it. However atrocious, it seems to me to be surpassed by many of the transactions in the Terra-firma, and it had at least the justification of being done in self-defence.* At last Morales and his men,

---

* If these captives, whom they stabbed and dropped, as

having fought their way with immense valour, if such a word can be justly applied to the proceedings of such men, and having had the most frightful difficulties and sufferings to contend with from the nature of the country they passed through, reached Darien. Pizarro was the second in command here; it certainly was a terrible school, in which to bring up the future conqueror of Peru.

All these expeditions had been so manifestly unsuccessful, that the Governor of Darien began to take the state of affairs much to heart. He ordered the melting-house, *Casa de la Fundicion,* to be closed—a most clear signal of distress; he also, in conjunction with the bishop, ordered public prayers to be offered up, that God might remove His anger from them. I do not find, however, that any change of policy took place in accordance with these prayers, unless it was that the next expedition seems to have been sent out in a different direction. But it, like the others, proved unsuccessful.

---

they went along, were the daughters and wives of the Indians, whom the Spaniards are represented as having captured in the midst of some festivity, it was an act of cruelty seldom equalled.

Then Espinosa, Pedrarias's alcalde mayor, had an opportunity of retrieving the fortunes of the colony, and restoring peace of mind to the governor. A monk, who accompanied the expedition, upon his return to Spain, stated that he had seen with his own eyes, killed by the sword or thrown to savage dogs, in this expedition of Espinosa's, above forty thousand souls. This seems almost incredible, but let no one doubt it, or imagine that he can realize to his mind what such an expedition would be capable of, until he has fully pictured to himself what his own nature might become, if he formed one of such a band, toiling in a new fierce clime, enduring miseries unimagined by him before, gradually giving up all civilized ways, growing more and more indifferent to the destruction of life,—the life of animals, of his adversaries, of his companions, even his own,—retaining the adroitness and sagacity of man, and becoming fell, reckless, and rapacious, as the fiercest brute of the forest. Not more different is the sea, when, some midsummer morning, it comes with its crisp, delicate little waves, fondling up to your feet, like your own dog,—and the same sea, when, storm-ridden, it thunders in against you with foam and fury like a wild beast; than is the smiling, prosperous, civilized man, restrained by a thousand invisible fetters, who has not known real hunger for years, from the same man, when he has starved and fought and bled, been alternately frozen and burned up, and when his life, in fact, has become one mad blinding contest with all around him.

Espinosa's expedition, however murderous, was not unsuccessful in the way in which success was then reckoned; for he recovered some gold, that had been lost on a previous expedition, and brought back eighty thousand *pesos* and two thousand slaves. Pascual de Andagoya, one of the captains in it, says that "all this company of slaves perished at Darien, as did all the rest who were brought there."

Throughout these expeditions in the Terra-firma, which would else be as interesting as they are important, the reader is vexed and distracted by new and uncouth names of people and of places. The very words Rome, Constantinople, London, Genoa, Venice stir the blood, and arrest the attention; any small incident in their fortunes enjoys some of the accumulated interest, which is bound up with these time-honoured names; while it requires an effort of imagination to care about what may happen to Comogra, Dabaye, Poncha, or Pocorosa. It is only on perceiving the immense importance of those events, which happen in the early days of new-found countries, that we can sufficiently arouse our attention to consider such events at all.

Then, however, we may see that the fate of future empires, and the distribution of races over the face of the earth depend upon the painful deeds of a few adventurers and unrenowned native chieftains; they themselves being like players, whose names and private fortunes we do not care much about, but who are acting in some great drama, the story of which concerns the whole world.

CHAPTER VI.

*Vasco Nuñez restless—sends for men on his own account.—
The Governor is angry.—Vasco Nuñez receives the title of
Adelantado from the Court of Spain—is reconciled to the
Governor, espouses his daughter—is sent by the Governor
to Acla to build ships for the Sea of the South—carries the
materials across the isthmus—is suspected by the Governor.
Pizarro is sent to arrest him.—Vasco Nuñez is tried, con-
victed of high treason, and executed.*

WHILE all those expeditions, which have
been mentioned in the previous chapter,
were being carried on, and in one of
which Pizarro was employed, it will not be supposed that Vasco Nuñez, with all his activity and
energy—a man of whom it had been said that
" he could not be quiet, while his bread was being
baked"—was patient or at rest. It has been seen
that he had become a critical observer of men's
actions; but looking on was not likely to satisfy
a man of his restless disposition.

Many and severe must have been the comparisons, made by the men who had served under him, between the successful mode, in which he had alternately soothed and terrified the Indian caciques, and the unsuccessful manner, in which the captains of Pedrarias had prosecuted their disastrous adventures. As, therefore, Pedrarias did not seem likely to employ him, he at length resolved to undertake an expedition of his own, and sent secretly to Cuba for men, to accompany him in peopling the coasts of the Southern Sea.

While his messenger, Andres Garavito, was away on this errand, Pedrarias, perhaps at the solicitation of the Bishop of Darien, or it might have been from motives of policy, resolved to employ him in making an entrance (a favourite phrase of the Spaniards) into the country of Dabaye, of which Vasco had written great accounts to the Court of Spain. But, encountering here the Indians on the water, he completely failed, got wounded, and escaped with difficulty. It may be imagined that this ill-success was not displeasing to the captains of Pedrarias, or, indeed, to the governor himself.

It was seen that Vasco Nuñez, soon after his

discovery of the South Sea, had sent a man named Arbolanche to the Court of Spain with the good news and with rich presents. This messenger did not come in time to stop the appointment of Pedrarias; but the tidings, which Arbolanche brought, were well received; and the king not only pardoned Vasco Nuñez, but conferred upon him the title of Adelantado. Hitherto it had been the fashion at the Court of Spain to speak very slightingly of Vasco Nuñez; but this intelligence of the discovery of the South Sea—the greatest that had reached the mother country, since Columbus had brought back the tidings and the signs of a new world,—must have changed in great measure the opinions of the King and of the Court respecting Vasco Nuñez. Joined with this title of Adelantado, the government of Coyva and Panamá was also granted to him. Coyva is a small island where Vasco Nuñez thought that there were pearls. The king did not omit to endeavour to make Pedrarias and Vasco Nuñez act harmoniously together, recommending the governor to show all kindness to so useful a servant of the Crown as Vasco Nuñez; and Vasco Nuñez to please Pedrarias as much as possible. But, as one of Vasco Nuñez's biographers observes, " that which was easy at court was impossible at Darien, where factions prevented it."

Not long after this time Andres Garavito, the messenger whom Vasco Nuñez had sent to Cuba, returned with seventy men, and all the necessary provisions for an expedition, and came to place himself under the orders of Vasco Nuñez. But, when at six leagues from the port, he sent secretly to advise Vasco Nuñez of his arrival; but the intelligence also reached the ears of the governor, who ordered Vasco Nuñez to be arrested and sent to prison. At the entreaty, however, of the Bishop of Darien, the governor did not send Vasco Nuñez to prison, but set him free on certain conditions, which were arranged between them.

Vasco Nuñez was now left for some time in neglect, and might have remained so, but for the interposition of the Bishop of Darien, between whom and Vasco Nuñez a strong friendship or alliance had sprung up. The bishop succeeded in making Vasco Nuñez and the governor friends, and he proposed to cement this friendship by the strongest family bonds, suggesting that Pedrarias should give his daughter in marriage to Vasco

Nuñez. The governor assented; the espousals were formally made; but the young lady herself was in Spain.

Pedrarias now sent Vasco Nuñez to occupy a town in the port of Acla, whence he was to prepare to embark upon the South Sea. Acla, however, was on one side of the Isthmus, and the South Sea on the other. It was the bold, and, considering the number of lives that were consumed by it, the cruel scheme of Vasco Nuñez to prepare for the construction of his vessels at Acla, and to carry the materials overland to the South Sea.

His first vessels, which were prepared only after unheard-of labour and terrific loss of life among the Indians, were rendered useless by the wood having been eaten through and through with worms. The next set, before they were completed, were partly swept away, partly buried in mud and slime by a high tide, which drove the terrified workmen up into the trees for safety. They failed, too, in obtaining food, so that Vasco Nuñez himself was obliged to live upon such roots of the earth, as he could get.

Receiving, however, fresh supplies from the

governor, the Adelantado with incredible labour contrived to build two brigantines; there were two more also, almost completed.

It happened that about this time a report had reached Acla that Pedrarias was to be superseded, and Lope de Sosa appointed Governor of the Terra-firma. This, which some time ago would have been most joyous news, was now most unwelcome; his fortunes and those of his future father-in-law being bound up together. Talking one evening with two friends, one named Valderrabano, and the other a clerigo, named Rodrigo Perez, about the news of Lope de Sosa's coming, Vasco Nuñez observed that Francis Garavito had better go to Acla to ask for the iron and pitch which we want, and if there is a new governor, he will probably receive us well; if Pedrarias should still be in power, he can let him know in what state we are, and he will provide what we want; and then we shall set out on our voyage, of which I hope the success will be such as we so much desire. This conversation was very innocent. But it happened that, as Vasco Nuñez was talking, it began to rain, and the sentinel took shelter under the eaves of the hut, where Vasco and his friends were sitting; and he heard just so much of the conversation, as would convey the idea to him that Vasco Nuñez proposed to his companions to go away with the ships, and make the expedition on their own account.

Meanwhile, Andres Garavito, having had a quarrel with Vasco Nuñez about the Indian woman, daughter of Careta, who was much beloved by Vasco Nuñez, revenged himself by informing the governor that Vasco Nuñez intended freeing himself from his command. It is probable, too, that by this time the governor had heard from Spain of a letter, which Vasco Nuñez had sent thither, bearing date the 16th October 1515, in which were the strongest expressions of blame respecting the conduct of the government and the character of the governor. In it he tells the king of the atrocities committed by the captains of Pedrarias, of their turning friendly Indians into watchful enemies, ravaging the country, branding slaves in the most reckless manner, and desolating the land to such an extent, that, as he justly prophesies, hereafter it will not be possible to find a remedy for it. He speaks of the confusion in the government, of the want of concert and unity of purpose, of the neglect of the king's *hacienda*. He then proceeds to give his opinion of the governor's character : " He is a man, in whom reign all the envy and covetousness in the world; he is wretched, when he sees that there is friendship between any persons of worth; it delights him to hear fables and chatter from one and the other; he is a man, who very lightly gives credit to evil counsels rather than to those of good; he is a person without any discretion and without any dexterity or talent for the affairs of government."*

Pedrarias could no longer contain himself. Fully bent upon revenge for all his real and fancied wrongs, he masters his fury sufficiently to write a crafty letter, to Vasco Nuñez, begging him to come to him at Acla, that they might confer together upon business. While the governor was planning this, Vasco Nuñez was quietly and serenely awaiting the return of his messenger, Francis Garavito, to bring him intelligence whether Lope de Sosa was about to supersede Pedrarias as governor. Whatever that answer might be, Vasco Nuñez might well feel assured of for-

---

* Nav. Col., tom. iii. p. 384.

tune.   If his father-in-law continued in power, he might be joined by new adventurers, and be sure of fresh supplies; if Lope de Sosa were coming, he would sail away with his trustful company, free from any superior, and confident in his future fortunes; the light of his unique renown throwing forwards a brilliant track in the future, along which he would sail to still bolder adventures and still greater discoveries.   And such, indeed, would have been the probable result, had he once more spread his sails upon the waters, which owned him for their great discoverer.   In that case, the conquest of Peru would not have troubled us much with the name or the deeds of the ignorant Pizarro, but would have been made by one fitted to govern and reconstruct, as well as to conquer.   It was a career, with which, in the opinions of the men of that age, the stars were certain to have much concern; and, accordingly, we learn that a Venetian astrologer and natural philosopher, called Micer Codro, who had come to those parts to see the world, had told Vasco Nuñez that, the year in which he should see a certain star, which the astrologer pointed out, in such a place of the heavens, he would run great risk of his life; but, if he escaped that danger, he would be the greatest and richest lord in all the Indies.

Walking one evening—an evening in the tropics, where Nature is so large and so gracious,—probably along the sea-shore, whence he could see his brigantines lying idly in the harbour, Vasco Nuñez looked up, and beheld his fateful star in the quarter of the heavens, which the astrologer had pointed out to him. In the merry mood of a man who is near his doom—what the Scotch call "fey,"—he turned to his attendants, and began to mock at the prophecy. "A sensible man, indeed, would he be, who should believe in diviners, especially in Micer Codro, who told me this and this (here he related the Italian's words of omen); and, behold, I see the star he spoke of, when I find myself with four ships and three hundred men on the Sea of the South, just about to navigate it." Though Vasco Nuñez did thus despise the prophecy, it was a very judicious one (there is no little wisdom sometimes in the words of charlatans, a wisdom built upon great knowledge of life); for men's fortunes come to a focus, or rather to a point, in the intersection of many curves of other lines and circumstances; and what is done by them then has life and warmth in it, and can be done then only. It was easy to perceive, even for a person less versed in the foibles and wild wishes of mankind than an astrologer would be, that Vasco Nuñez was rapidly nearing some such crisis in his stormy life.

It will be inferred also that this was a great crisis, too, in the life of Pizarro; if Vasco succeeded, Pizarro would be compelled to be content to play a subordinate part for ever. In that case he would lose much glory, but would also escape much infamy; for every child, in connecting the name of Pizarro with Peru, has learned to think of him, as the destroyer of thousands of unoffending and unresisting Indians. It is not quite clear that Pizarro saw that the rising of Vasco Nuñez's star was the declining of his own, but undoubtedly he felt that, as long as Vasco Nuñez was on the stage, his part was merely secondary. At any rate he had separated himself from Vasco and his fortunes; indeed, from the time of Enciso's return with Pedrarias, Pizarro seems to have sided with those, who were hostile to Vasco Nuñez. It must be remembered that Enciso came out as alguazil mayor under Pedrarias, and we shall soon see proofs of the intimate connection, that lay at this time between Pizarro and Enciso, the implacable enemy of Vasco Nuñez.

While Vasco Nuñez was contemplating his future fortunes in such a confident spirit, he was little aware that the sleepless furies were even then close behind him. Dramatically, at that very moment when he was gazing upon his star in the fateful quarter of the heavens; really, a few days afterwards, a messenger from Pedrarias brought a treacherous letter to him in the Island of Tortoises. No one sent a word of warning to him, not even his own messenger at Acla; perhaps the governor had confided to no one his real intent. Vasco Nuñez went with the utmost readiness to meet his father-in-law at Acla. Now at least, two men must have known of the governor's intent to arrest him, and those were the alguazil mayor, Enciso, and Francisco Pizarro; the latter of whom was sent out from Acla with soldiers on the road to meet Vasco Nuñez, and seize his person. When Vasco Nuñez saw Pizarro and the soldiers waiting to arrest him, he exclaimed, " What is this, Francisco Pizarro, you were not

wont to come out in this fashion to receive me?"
But he attempted neither flight nor resistance;
and, being thus taken, he was put into the house
of a man, called Casteneda, while the Licentiate
Espinosa was ordered to proceed against him with
all rigour. It is worth remarking that this very
Espinosa was afterwards a silent partner with Pizarro, in furnishing out the expedition to Peru.

At first, Pedrarias pretended that Espinosa was
to proceed against Vasco Nuñez only to give him
an opportunity of justifying himself; but, afterwards, he showed his true wishes, and broke out
into violent reproaches against his son-in-law, who
protested that he was innocent of the meditated
offence laid to his charge, asking why should he
have come to Acla to meet Pedrarias, if he had
not been conscious of his innocence? It was not
difficult to form a good indictment against Vasco
Nuñez, introducing the imprisonment of Enciso,
the death of Nicuesa, and the reported conversation of Vasco Nuñez with his friends, partially
overheard by the sentinel, which must have been
the main ground of the charge. Vasco denies the
treason imputed to him. Witnesses are sought
for to prove the crimes which he has committed;

his words from the beginning are collected (this is the point at which a friend's hostility, i. e. if it is held that Andres Garavito, his former friend and ally, had turned against him, would be so fatal), and his offence is judged to be worthy of death. The Licentiate Espinosa, in giving a report to Pedrarias of the result of the process, said that Vasco Nuñez had incurred the penalty of death, but, taking into consideration the eminent services, which he had rendered to the state, the licentiate recommended that his life should be spared. Pedrarias, however, was implacable. " Since he has sinned, let him die for it," was the exclamation of the fiery old man ; and he ordered the sentence to be instantly carried into effect, which was that they should cut off Vasco Nuñez's head, the crier going before him, and saying with a loud voice, " This is the justice, which our lord the King, and Pedrarias, his lieutenant, in his name, command to be done upon this man, as a traitor and usurper of the lands subject to the royal crown." It was in vain that Vasco Nuñez protested against the sentence. He was beheaded, and after him four of his friends, who were implicated in the so-called conspiracy ; among whom was the lay friend Valderrabano, to whom he confided his intentions on that evening, which proved so fatal to him. The Clerigo, probably on account of his profession, escaped a like fate.

Thus perished Vasco Nuñez de Balboa, in the forty-second year of his age; the man, who, since the time of Columbus, had shown the most states-man-like and warrior-like powers in that part of the world, but whose career was cut short, before he had had time to do more than to follow in the paths of Ojeda, and Nicuesa, and the other unfor-tunate commanders, who devastated those beautiful regions of the earth. He had helped to pull down, and was cut off, before he had the opportunity to attempt to reconstruct, and reorganize. But, at least, his death left the path to Peru open to Pizarro, though not immediately; for Vasco Nuñez was beheaded A.D. 1517, but it was not until November, A.D. 1524, that Pizarro sailed upon his first expedition to Peru. An interval of seven years has to pass by, and during those years, in the restless eagerness of the Spaniards on the Isthmus for discoveries, it seems wonderful that Peru should not have yielded up herself before that.

BOOK THE SECOND.

CHAPTER I.

Pedrarias uses Vasco Nuñez's ships—Espinosa sent out—
Gil Gonçalez—The Spice Islands—Lope de Sosa dies—
Pizarro takes to cattle farming—Almagro his partner—
Nicaragua—Panamá—Hernandez de Cordova sent against
Gil Gonçalez—Pascual de Andagoya's Expedition towards
Peru—Juan de Basarto is allowed to make a voyage to-
wards Peru—Dies—Pizarro and Almagro come forward—
The triumvirate.

IT was not likely that Pedrarias would leave those ships, which Vasco Nuñez had constructed with such incredible toil, and which, at his death, were lying ready at anchor in the Sea of the South, unemployed. As soon, however, as the news of Vasco Nuñez's execution reached Spain, Gil Gonçalez Davila, who had formerly been attached to the household of the Bishop of Burgos, received permission to use those ships on a proposed expedition to the Spice Islands. This was done on the supposition that Lope de Sosa would supersede Pedrarias as Governor of Darien. But Lope de Sosa never reached Darien alive; Pedrarias, therefore, continued governor: but, even before the death of Lope de Sosa, which happened A. D. 1518, the covetous old man had not failed to take advantage of Vasco Nuñez's death, and to make use of his preparations for discovery in the South Sea. The Licentiate Espinosa, the very man who had the charge of the prosecution of Vasco Nuñez, was sent by him to take possession of his ships, and to see whether anything could be made out of his designs. A great mistake was here made in not joining Pizarro with this expedition; for what, in Vasco Nuñez's hands, or indeed under Pizarro, would have ended in the discovery of Peru, now turned out a fruitless enterprise. Espinosa, instead of going south, where he would have come upon Peru, went northwards; and returned with only having discovered a small extent of country, as far as Cape Blanco.

Gil Gonçalez, although disappointed in finding

the government of Darien still in the hands of Pedrarias, and Vasco Nuñez's ships occupied in an expedition, did not give up his idea, but persevered in preparing other ships on the South Sea; and at last, in January, 1522, set sail from an island in the Gulf of San Miguel, in order to discover the Spice Islands. It is singular to notice how no one at this time thought of anything, but the Spice Islands. It seemed to all, both to the monarchs of Spain, to their statesmen, and to their captains, that the most desirable enterprise, which maritime daring could accomplish for their nation, was the discovery of these Spice Islands. It is that idea, undoubtedly, which reserved Peru for Pizarro, who at this time had not sufficient influence to obtain the command of any public expedition, and had not means at his disposal to furnish out one at his private expense. He must, however, have felt that whatever he wished to do must be done at his own private cost; for, keeping the report of Peru and her riches, which he had heard from the mouth of Comogre's son, in mind, he took to cattle farming. His partner in this occupation was a man named Almagro.

The land of Kublai Khan was not more attractive to Columbus, than the Spice Islands to the Spanish sovereigns. Gil Gonçalez therefore set out, bent on discovering them. The notions, which the Spaniards had of geography, must have been somewhat limited and incorrect, for they turned their course to the north-west instead of to the south-west. That saved Peru. They discovered the whole coast of Nicaragua, and made considerable incursions into the interior. The discoveries on the southern side of the Isthmus were now considerable; and Pedrarias, taking advantage of Espinosa's small discovery on the north-west coast, claimed the whole of Gil Gonçalez's newly-discovered country, Nicaragua; and, that he might be nearer the spot to maintain his rights, established an important station at Panamá, on the southern side of the Isthmus,—a proceeding of the utmost importance in facilitating the conquest of Peru; for, without a station of some magnitude on the southern side, whence supplies of food and reinforcements could easily be drawn, the conquest of a large country like Peru would have been almost impossible. It was here, at Panamá, that Pizarro and Almagro had their *repartimientos* of Indians, and here their cattle-farms were. The old governor met with no little trouble in asserting his right to the government of Nicaragua; for his captain, Francisco Hernandez de Córdova, after driving out Gil Gonçalez, wished to free himself from Pedrarias's authority, and to hold his command directly from the *audiencia* of Hispaniola, at whose head was Don Diego Columbus, the son of the great discoverer. These auditors were, theoretically, the most powerful body in the New World. Pedrarias, however, proceeded at once into Nicaragua, and held a courtmartial on his unfortunate lieutenant; who made no attempt to escape, and was forthwith convicted and beheaded, A. D. 1526.

The idea of an expedition to Peru had not been during this time altogether abandoned; for Pascual de Andagoya, one of Espinosa's captains, with Espinosa's assistance, obtained the consent of the governor to a voyage in the " Sea of the South," in the year 1522. He had an encounter with the natives of Birú, and, it is said, reduced seven of the lords of the country into obedience to the king of Spain. He gained additional knowledge of the coast southwards, which he afterwards imparted to Pizarro. Meeting, however, with an accident which disabled him, he returned to Panamá. The attention of the governor was now taken up with his conquest of Nicaragua; and he would hear of nothing else. But when Gil Gonçalez had been driven out a certain man named Juan Basarto, to whom Pedrarias was under obligation for his having brought men and horses to aid in the Nicaraguan conquest, came forward and requested to be allowed to make an expedition to Peru. The governor consented, but Juan de Basarto died; this was early in 1524. It was at this juncture that Pizarro and Almagro, having made a considerable sum of money by their cattle-farming, came forward and offered to take up the expedition. This Almagro, of whom a great deal will be heard from this time forward, was the son of a labouring man, with no taint, however, of Moorish or Jewish blood, bred up in a town belonging to the Order of Calatrava. Impatient of a labourer's life, he had taken service with a licentiate who lived at the Court of Ferdinand and Isabella. It happened that, in a quarrel with another youth, he stabbed him; and, not daring to await his trial, he fled, wandering hither and thither, until finally he came to the Indies, and was one of the soldiers employed under Pedrarias. Almagro was, however, in character totally dissimilar to his partner Pizarro. While Pizarro was slow, taciturn, reserved, Almagro was alert, impulsive, generous, and wonderfully skilled in gaining the hearts of men. They had, some little time before, taken into partnership (undoubtedly with a view to an expedition at their own private cost to the Sea of the South), a very different person to themselves, named Fernando de Luque, a *clerigo* and a schoolmaster. This *clerigo* was a favourite with the Governor Pedrarias, and had a much better *repartimiento* than the other partners, situated close to theirs, on the bank of the river Chagre, four leagues from Panamá. It has been discovered in modern times that the Licentiate Espinosa, the prosecutor of the unfortunate Vasco Nuñez, was also a silent partner, and that it was on his account principally that De Luque joined the partnership. At any rate, the resources of De Luque, the steady management of Pizarro, and the keen activity of Almagro made the partnership a prosperous concern. By their cattle-farms they realized fifteen or eighteen thousand *pesos* of gold; and well would it have been for all of them, had they been contented to remain as country gentlemen.   But their cattle-farming was but the means to an end.   And, therefore, when Juan de Basarto died, these three men came forward and offered to undertake his expedition; and that was no less than the conquest of Peru. The agreement between the partners was, that the division of profits should be equal.*   The division of labour is well stated by Garcilaso de la Vaga, when he says that Fernando de Luque was to remain in Panamá, to take care and make the most of the property of the three associates; Pizarro was to undertake the discovery and conquest; Almagro was to go and come, bringing supplies of men and arms to Pizarro, and then returning to De Luque, thus making himself the medium of communication between Panamá and Peru.   This company was much laughed at then, and the schoolmaster got the name of *Fernando el loco* (Fernando the Madman), though the triumvirate was afterwards compared to the memorable

* Pedrarias afterwards became a partner in the enterprize, and was to receive a fourth of the profits.

Roman one of Lepidus, Marc Antony, and Octavius. It was remarked at the time, and intended to be a sarcasm, that these Spanish triumvirs were all elderly men (Pizarro was now fifty-four years old); but the remark was not a very wise one, for it has never been found that ambition or the love of novelty dies out of the human heart at any certain age. All men, too, are but children in those things which they have not experienced; and not one of these three associates had been what he would have called a successful man. The disappointed are ever young; at least, they are as anxious to undertake new things, as the most hopeful among the young. Moreover, the principal partner, Pizarro, was haunted by a fixed idea, namely, the discovery of rich regions in the southern seas,—the words of Comogre's son had been a sort of light beckoning him for ever on to riches and to fame; he had witnessed the attempts of others to grasp what he knew lay in the unknown south, and each time fortune had struck them down, or diverted them away. The south lay for *him;* and advancing years only lent a fiercer aspect to this idea, as they narrowed him in, and left less and less time for its development.

CHAPTER II.

Pizarro sets sail—his difficulties—is wounded—recommences his voyage—his dispute with Almagro—some of his men leave him—his sufferings—succour comes—Tumbez—he receives two young Indians—returns to Panamá.

THE voyage of Pizarro is only second to that of Columbus himself. There may have been voyages in the history of the world more important and more interesting than that of Pizarro; but if so, the details of them have been lost. The voyage of Cortes from Cuba to the coast of Mexico was but a slight affair in the history of that man's remarkable proceedings; but, in Pizarro's life, the voyage is the greatest part of the career.

The preparations for the outfit were commenced in 1524. A vessel was bought, which, it is said, had been built by Vasco Nuñez de Balboa; and another was put upon the stocks. The expenses were very great. Each shipwright received two golden *pesos* a day, and his food. Moreover, it was not possible to go into the market-place, or down upon the sea-shore, and enlist at once as many soldiers or sailors as might be wanted; but the partners had gradually to form their complement of men, providing food and lodgment for them when hired, watching for new comers from Castille, taking care of them in the illnesses to which they were liable on first coming into the country, and advancing them small sums of money, probably to clear them from debt. At last the preparations were complete. The three partners, Pizarro, Almagro, and De Luque, heard mass together, and rendered the compact more solemn by each partaking of the sacrament: and, about the middle of November, 1524, Pizarro set sail in one vessel, with two canoes, containing eighty men and four horses. A treasurer, Nicolas de Rivera, and an inspector, Juan Carillo, who was to look after the king's fifths, accompanied the expedition. Almagro was to follow in the other vessel, with more men and provisions.

Pizarro touched at the island of Taboga, took

in wood and water at the Pearl Islands, and arrived at the Puerto de Pinas. From thence he made an expedition into the Cacique Birú's country. This was a land which, from its rough and difficult nature, was very difficult to conquer or to occupy. It was a great error to have stopped there at all: but probably Pizarro did not wish to go too far, for fear of missing the promised reinforcement that was to come with Almagro.

It may show the difficulties under which the expedition was got up by these men, when we find Pizarro in his one ship, with eighty men, enduring for the next three months when Almagro joined them, the most dreadful privations. It seems as if the partners thought anything was better than deferring the starting of the expedition until larger means had been procured, or returning discomfited to Panamá. For here they were in a desert or deserted country, suffering incredibly from hunger, and finding nothing worthy of all this suffering. They proceeded ten leagues down the coast, and arrived at a port which they called Puerto de la Hambre, the Port of Hunger. Nothing was to be got there but wood and water. They again sailed on for ten successive days. The provisions they had brought with them were growing less and less, and finally the rations appointed for each man were but two ears of maize a day. Water also began to fail them. The more impatient of the crew talked of returning to Panamá. Pizarro, with a power of endurance and a mildness that belonged to his character, and which he must have often seen exercised by Vasco Nuñez under similar circumstances, did his best to console his men, and to encourage them by the high hopes that steadily remained before his wistful eyes. They turned back, however, and made their way to the Puerto de la Hambre. They did not lose heart even yet; and now Pizarro resolved to stop at this deplorable Puerto, and send back the ship to the Pearl Islands, to seek for provisions. Neither for those who stayed nor for those who went, were there any provisions but the dried hide of a cow and the bitter palm-buds which are gathered on that coast. This was the same food that Pizarro had known in early days, when he was left as Ojeda's lieutenant at San Sebastian. He was, however always on the alert, endeavouring to provide any sustenance however wretched, for his sick men; and his constant mind betrayed not the slightest sign of being overcome by adversity. In labours and dangers he was ever the first. Did any expedition promise advantage or help, Pizarro would not give to anyone else the labour, but undertook the management of everything himself. The Indians of these parts had poison for their arrows. The Spaniards saw a man die of a wound in four hours. Had the herb from which this poison is distilled been found lower down the coast, upon the broad plains beyond Tumbez, the conquest of Peru would hardly have been made in that generation.

Pizarro's ship now returned from the Pearl Islands with some provisions. But the number of Spaniards who died of hunger at the Puerto de la Hambre was twenty-seven.

The whole body now recommenced their voyage, and went further down the coast. Landing at a place which they called the *Pueblo Quemado*, they came, at the distance of about a league from the shore, upon a deserted Indian town, situated on an eminence and having the appearance of a fortress. They found also plenty of provisions here. The town being near the sea, well-placed for defence, and well provisioned, it seemed to Pizarro and his men that they might prudently make a station here. Their only vessel leaked, and they resolved to send it back to Panamá to get it repaired; but before this Pizarro ordered an incursion to be made, in order to secure the persons of some of the Indians. The Indians retreated before the attacking party, and, knowing the country well, made a circuit, and came down upon Pizarro and his few men who had remained in the town. Pizarro, an able man-at-arms, withstood the attack bravely, and made himself a general mark for the Indians. They pressed upon him, wounded him, and he fell down a steep descent. They followed, but before they could kill him he was upon his legs again, and able to defend himself. Some of his men rushed to his assistance. The rest of the Spaniards now returned, and compelled the enemy to take to flight.

They then resolved to quit the *Pueblo Quemado*, finding that the Indians were too many for them, and to return with their ship towards Panamá.

Throughout this extraordinary voyage the Spaniards were not fortunate enough to come upon any Indian settlement that was suitable for them.

Sometimes there were too many Indians in the vicinity; more often there were too few.

Arriving at Chicamá, in the government of the Terra-firma, they sent from thence the treasurer of the expedition, Nicolas de Rivera, in their vessel with the gold they had found, to give an account to the Governor Pedrarias of what they had done and suffered, and of the hopes they still had of making some great discovery. Meanwhile, they remained at Chicamá, a humid, melancholy, sickly spot, where it rained continually.

Almagro, always active, had not forgotten his part of the undertaking; and starting three months after Pizarro had set out, came in search of him with the other vessel belonging to the associates. When Nicolas de Rivera brought up at the Island of Pearls, he learned that Almagro had passed, and he sent to Pizarro to inform him of this joyful intelligence. Proceeding to Panamá, Rivera informed Pedrarias of what had happened. The governor was angry when he heard of the death of the many Spaniards who had already perished in the expedition. He blamed Pizarro for his pertinacity; and the schoolmaster, De Luque, had much difficulty in preventing the governor from joining another person in command with Pizarro.

Meanwhile Almagro pursued his way down the coast, making diligent search for Pizarro. The only traces he could find of him were the marks of the Spanish hatchets, where the men had landed to cut wood. At last he made an entrance into that part of the country which had already been so unfortunate for the Spaniards— in the neighbourhood of the *Pueblo Quemado*. He found this town inhabited, and fortified with palisades. He resolved to take it, and, accordingly, commenced the attack with great vigour. The Indians defended themselves obstinately. Almagro was wounded in the right eye by a dart, and was so pressed upon by the Indians, that he would have been left for dead, if he had not been rescued by a negro slave of his. Notwithstanding his sufferings he renewed the contest, and at last succeeded in gaining the place. His men were greatly distressed at the accident which had befallen their leader. They placed him on a litter made of branches of trees, and when the pain was assuaged they bore him back to his vessel.

Again they proceeded on their voyage, and arrived at the river of San Juan, where the country seemed better than any they had passed, and where, on both banks of the river, there were Indian settlements. They did not venture to land, however, and resolved to return to Panamá. Touching at the Island of Pearls on their way back, they learnt that the treasurer, Rivera, had passed that way, and had left word that Pizarro was at Chicamá. Almagro's delight at hearing this was great. He had supposed that his companion was dead. He returned to Chicamá and found him. The two commanders recounted their misfortunes to each other, but resolved to persevere in their undertaking. It was arranged that Almagro should return to Panamá, while Pizarro was to maintain his men in the melancholy spot where he then was.

Almagro found Pedrarias very ill-disposed towards the expedition. He was at that time about to enter Nicaragua, in order to chastise his lieutenant, Francisco Hernandez de Córdova, and was not inclined to spare any more men for the expedition to Peru. Again, however, De Luque persuaded Pedrarias not to withhold his licence for the levy of more men, though the governor remained still so much displeased with Pizarro, that he would not leave him the sole leader of the enterprise, but joined Almagro with him in the supreme command. Almagro, with two ships, and two canoes, with arms, provisions, and a pilot named Bartolomé Ruiz, set sail from Panamá, and joined Pizarro at the place where he had left him. Pizarro felt deeply the slur cast upon his command by Almagro's being joined with him in it, and this has been considered* to have been the commencement of the ill feeling between the two friends.

The enterprise was prosecuted with renewed vigour. The two commanders went down the coast, and arrived at a river, which they called the River Cartagena, near to the San Juan. Thence they made a sudden attack upon one of the towns on the River San Juan, in which they were successful; for they captured some Indians, and took some gold, weighing fifteen thousand *pesos*, of an inferior description. They also found provisions there. Returning to their ships, they determined to divide their forces. Almagro was to return to

---

* See Quintana's *Life of Pizarro.*

Panamá for more men. Bartolomé Ruiz, the pilot, was to prosecute discovery along the coast. Pizarro was to remain with his men where they were.

These resolutions were immediately carried into execution. Bartolomé Ruiz, a very dexterous pilot, was exceedingly successful in his share of the enterprise. He discovered the Island of Gallo, went on to the Bay of San Mateo, and thence to Coaque. Still pursuing his course in a south-westerly direction, he descried, to his great astonishment, in the open sea, a large object which seemed like a caravel, and had a lateen sail. He made for this object and discovered that it was a raft. He captured it,* and found two young men and three women. Interrogating them by signs, he ascertained that they

---

* Almagro afterwards gave an account to Oviedo of various things, that were found on board this Peruvian vessel, and they were such, as greatly to increase the confidence of Almagro in the ultimate success of his undertaking. There were pottery on board, and woollen clothes of exquisite workmanship, also silver and gold; and the crew spoke of carrying with them a test-stone for gold, and a steel-yard for weighing it and other metals.

were natives of a place called Tumbez. They
spoke many times of a king, Huayna Capac, and
of Cusco, where there was much gold. Bartolomé Ruiz went on, passed the equinoctial line,
and arrived at a town called Zalongo. From
thence he retured to Pizarro.

This commander and his men needed all the
comfort, that Ruiz could give them by the
favourable intelligence which he brought. It
was always the business of Pizarro patiently to
endure great suffering, and to sustain the men
under his command in the most abject kind of
adversity. During the absence of Bartolomé
Ruiz they had suffered from sickness and hunger;
their clothes were never dry; they had been un-
ceasingly plagued by mosquitos, and had been
attacked, and some of them devoured, by *caymans*.
The Indians had not left them unmolested, and
fourteen of the Spaniards had died at the hands of
the natives.

It was now far advanced in the year 1526, and
Pedro de los Rios had arrived to supersede
Pedrarias. And Pedrarias demanded four thousand
pesos as his price for ceasing to be a partner in the
expedition.

After some angry bargaining he consented to give up all his claims for a thousand *pesos*, to be paid him at a certain date. This buying Pedrarias out shows the extreme confidence which, even at a time of great depression and disappointment, Almagro at least, had in the ultimate success of his undertaking.

Almagro too found favour with the new governor so far as to gain his permission to enlist soldiers. Having enlisted about forty, he set sail with the requisite provisions from Panamá, and joined Pizarro at the river San Juan.

They all re-embarked, intent upon prosecuting the discovery which Bartolomé Ruiz had already commenced. They stopped at the Island of Gallo, to refit, passed the bay of San Mateo, and went down the coast to a town called Tacamez; but a little plunder, here and there, at the expense of much toil, distress, and sacrifice of health and life, was the only result.

At this point there was a good deal of hesitation as to their future course, and discussion as to what should be done. It is said that Pizarro was for returning, no doubt dissatisfied with what appeared to be a mere marauding expedition, and one not at all equal to the task of discovering and conquering the rich countries Comogre's son had spoken of; but Almagro was for pursuing the plan that had already been so often adopted, namely, that he should return for more men to Panamá. It must not be thought that Pizarro, by counselling the return of the expedition to Panamá, had lost confidence in the object he had so long in view; it is more likely that he was convinced of the inefficiency of their present means, and was willing to risk imprisonment for debt at Panamá rather than waste any more time in unhealthy stations on the coast, waiting for the scanty supplies Almagro could collect at Panamá. Almagro thought that their present life was better than dying in prison for the debts they had already contracted. Pizarro replied that Almagro had not suffered from hunger as he had done, otherwise he also would counsel return. Upon this Almagro offered to change places, suggesting that Pizarro should go for reinforcements, while he remained to take charge of the men: Pizarro refused: high words passed between them, and swords were drawn. At this juncture the treasurer Rivera, and the pilot Bartolomé Ruiz interposed, and the old friends were reconciled.   Pizarro and his men were to stay in the island of Gallo, while Almagro returned again to Panamá.

But while the two captains Pizarro and Almagro, each in their different ways, were firmly bent upon doing something in the South, the common soldiers were heartily sick of the whole affair. One of them contrived to send to the governor of Panamá a petition concealed in a ball of cotton, in which he gave an account of their losses by death, and of their sufferings, and concluded his petition with some words which afterwards obtained a great renown in the Indies, and were in the mouths of all men there.

Literally translated they run thus—

> My good Lord Governor,
>   Have pity on our woes;
> For here remains the butcher,
>   To Panamá the salesman goes.

The governor, accordingly, sent a lawyer name Tafur to the Island of Gallo, to authorize the return of all those men under Pizarro's command who wished to make their way back to Panamá.

Under these circumstances, it was not to be expected that Almagro would be able to gain any new recruits. The governor's representative Tafur reached the island of Gallo, and the greater part of Pizarro's company prepared to depart. Pizarro addressed some words to his men, which Herrera justly describes as characterized by a singular modesty and constancy, and the historian might have added, by great prudence also. Pizarro said, that those who wished to return should by all means do so; but that it grieved him to think that they were going to endure greater sufferings and worse poverty than they had already endured, and to lose that which they had so long toiled for, as he did not doubt that they were on the point of discovering something which would console and enrich them all. He then reminded them of what those Indians had said whom Bartolomé Ruiz had captured. Finally, he observed that it gave him very great satisfaction to reflect that, in all they had undergone, he had not excused himself from being the principal sufferer, contriving that he should rather want than that they should,—and so, he said, it would always be.

The dire pressure, however, of recent suffering,

and a hungry desire to see home again, were too strong to be overcome by the wise and encouraging words of Pizarro. The men accordingly begged Tafur to take them away with him immediately. This lieutenant, however, pitying the straits to which Pizarro was reduced, gave him a chance of retaining any of his companions, who, at the last moment, might be unwilling to leave their brave old commander. Tafur, therefore, placed himself at one end of his vessel; and, drawing a line, put Pizarro and his men at the other. He then said, that those who wished to return to Panamá should pass over the line, and come to him, and those who did not wish to return should stay where they were, by the side of Pizarro. Fourteen resolute men, amongst whom was a mulatto, stood by the side of their chief; the rest passed over the line to Tafur.

This simple story has been told in a very different way, according to the invincible passion for melo-dramatic representation which people of second-rate imagination delight in, those especially who have not seen much of human affairs and who do not know in how plain and unpretending a manner the greatest things are, for the most part, transacted. The popular story is one which may remind the classical reader of the story of the choice of Hercules. Assembling his men, Pizarro drew his sword, and marked with it a line upon the sand from west to east. Then, pointing towards the south, the way to Peru, he said, " Gentlemen, on that side are labour, hunger, thirst, fatigue, wounds, sicknesses, and all the other dangers which have to be undergone until life is ended. Those who have the courage to endure these things and to be my faithful companions, let them pass the line. Those who feel themselves unworthy of so great an enterprise, let them return to Panamá, for I wish to force no man." Unfortunately for the credit of this story we have the evidence, taken before a judge, of one of the fourteen brave men who stayed with Pizarro, who states simply that " Pizarro being in the island of Gallo, the governor Rios sent for the men who were with the said captain, allowing any one who should wish to prosecute the enterprise to remain with him."

It matters but little, however, to show the exact form which the transaction took, except that it proves more for the good sense of those men who stayed with Pizarro, that they should have been induced to do so by the rational arguments which he held out to them, and by a constancy of purpose based upon due consideration of the facts, rather than by any momentary enthusiasm, the offspring of a sudden and dramatic incident. The most notable men among the fourteen were Pedro de Candia (a native of the island of Candia), and Bartolomé Ruiz de Moguer, the pilot of the expedition.

The rest of Pizarro's men went back with Tafur to Panamá, having endured a fearful amount of unrequited suffering,—having, as it were, watched through the darkest hours of the night, and not being able to abide that last cold hour before the sun makes its welcome appearance.

Pizarro and his fourteen brave companions did not venture to stay in the island of Gallo, as it was close to the shore, and could, therefore, be easily attacked by the Indians; but they went over to an uninhabited island, six leagues from land, called Gorgona. There, while waiting for supplies from Almagro, Pizarro and his men subsisted upon shell-fish, and whatever things in any way eatable they could collect upon the shore.

In the midst of all their misery they did not forget their piety. " Every morning they gave thanks to God: at evening-time they said the *Salve* and other prayers appointed for different hours. They took heed of the feasts of the Church, and kept account of their Fridays and Sundays." Indeed, the old Spanish proverb,

> " Si quereis saber orar,
> Aprended á navegar," [*]

was thoroughly exemplified in the conduct of Pizarro and his men while staying in the inhospitable island of Gorgona, " which those who have seen it compare with the infernal regions."

Meanwhile, the generous Almagro and the good De Luque did not forget their suffering partner left on the island. After repeated applications, they persuaded the governor to send a vessel for Pizarro. Pedro de los Rios consented, but attached to his consent the condition that Pizarro and his men should return in six months, or be subject to heavy penalties. Here then was the turning point in Pizarro's history, as dis-

---

[*] " Learn to be a sailor, if you would know how to pray."

coverer and conqueror of Peru. If the vessel that now came for him and his men took them back to Panamá, as men who had failed, the chances were that Pizarro at least would either die in prison, or live to see others reaping the results of all his patient and persevering labours. The vessel drew near: the men for joy, although they knew it was a sail, could not believe their eyes. At last, not even timidity itself could doubt; but it was not men, but supplies only, that were brought; and the command to return, under a severe penalty, in six months. In despair Pizarro and his men resolved to make the most use of the time which was allowed them. They set sail southwards, keeping close to the shore, and after twenty days came in sight of a little island which was opposite to Tumbez, and to which they gave the name of Santa Clara.

This island was a sacred spot whither at certain times the inhabitants of the mainland came to make sacrifices. The Spaniards landed and saw a stone idol having the figure of a man, except that its head was fashioned in a conical form. A much more satisfactory sight was to be seen in the rich offerings of precious metal which were there—pieces of gold and silver wrought in the shape of hands, women's breasts, and heads; a large silver jug, which held four gallons of water; also beautifully woven woollen mantles, dyed yellow, the mourning colour of the Peruvians. The natives whom Bartolomé Ruiz had captured said that these riches were nothing compared to those that were to be found in their country.

The Spaniards embarked again, and the next day discovered a great raft with some of the natives upon it. Then again, four other rafts. Pizarro made them return with him to Tumbez, and when they arrived there, he gave them leave to depart, and entrusted them with a friendly message to the chief inhabitants of Tumbez.

It was resolved in Tumbez to be hospitable to the strangers, and to send a present to them under the conduct of a man in authority, whom, from the artificial deformity of his ears (a sign of rank), the Spaniards called an *Orejon.*

Friendly discourse passed between Pizarro and this *Orejon.* They dined together, and afterwards the Spanish captain gave him some presents—an iron hatchet, some strings of pearls, and three chalcedones. To the principal lord of the town he sent two swine and some fowls. The Orejon asked if Pizarro would permit some of his men to return with him to the town. Pizarro consented, and a certain Alonzo de Molina, with a negro, accompanied the Orejon on shore.

The principal lord of Tumbez was astonished at the new animals which Pizarro had sent him. When the cock crowed he asked what it said. But nothing surprised him or his people so much as the negro. They endeavoured to wash him. The bystanders little thought that these two strangers —the Spaniard and the negro—were the representatives of nations who came to dispossess them, and that thousands upon thousands of these black men would become in after days the inhabitants of their dear Peru.   On the other hand, the Spaniard and the negro were not less astonished at what they beheld. They saw a fortress which had six or seven walls, aqueducts, stone houses, vessels of silver and gold.   Indeed they had now arrived at a spot where they might form some estimate of Peruvian civilization.   The valley of Tumbez contained a town, where was a palace of the reigning Inca, a temple dedicated to the sun, where were the sacred virgins; and beautiful gardens, in which all kinds of plants and animals were kept. Some of these animals gave occasion to what was looked upon as a miracle of no small importance. Pizarro, wishing to test the accuracy of Molina's account of what he had seen, sent Pedro de Candia, a large man of noble presence, to see the town. Clad in a coat of mail, with a brazen shield on his left arm, his sword in his belt, and in his right hand a wooden cross, the bold Greek stepped forth towards the town, as if he had been the lord of the whole province. The people flocked to see him, and wishing, very judiciously, to ascertain the temper and quality of their new guest, let loose two wild animals (a lion and tiger they are called); but these animals, perhaps too well fed to attack any man, especially one clad in mail, made no attempt to molest him; while he, as the story goes, made no attempt to frighten them, but gently laid the cross upon their backs, " thus giving those Gentiles to understand that the virtue of that sign took away the ferocity even of wild beasts." What effect it had hitherto had upon men was not so clearly signified. The natives now received Pedro de Candia as a superior being, and conducted him over the temple and the palace. The temple was lined with plates of gold, and the palace contained every kind of vessel for use and ornament made of the same precious metal. In the gardens were animals moulded in gold. Pedro de Candia, having feasted his eyes with these splendours, returned to his companions. They now knew enough of the riches of Peru to satisfy the most incredulous; but they still persevered in going down the coast. They reached Collaque and went on farther to what they called Puerto de Santa. But, having reconnoitred thus far, they resolved to return to Panamá. In all this region they were well received by the natives. Pizarro had the prudence to ask for some young Indians to be given him, who might be taught the Castillian language. Two youths were accordingly brought to him, who were baptized, one being named Martin and the other Felipillo (little Philip), who afterwards became a celebrated and most mischievous interpreter. The gallant company then made their way back to Panamá freighted with great news. Peru had been discovered. What Comogre's son had years before this told Vasco Nuñez was proved to be quite true, the Spaniards might indeed *here* fulfil their desires, and *here* were the precious metals in greater abundance than was iron in Biscay; but what he at the same time said was true also, that a thousand men would be requisite for undertaking the conquest of this country. The next thing then that Pizarro determined upon was to obtain these thousand men and effect the conquest.

He had at least returned a successful man. His patience and indomitable perseverance had so far brought their reward. Whoever might gain the advantage of the conquest of Peru, he had been the discoverer of it. And so he returned to Panamá; not satisfied, but so far successful as to be in a position to ask for what shall ensure success. This was at the end of the year 1527.

CHAPTER III.

*Pizarro goes to the Spanish Court—Returns to Panamá—
Starts for the Conquest of Peru—Is again surrounded with
difficulties—Founds the town of San Miguel.*

PIZARRO, immediately upon his arrival
at Panamá, determined to go at once
to the Spanish Court, in order to get
established, if possible, in his rights as discoverer of Peru, and to obtain men and means to
effect the conquest of it. He thought that
Comogre's son's thousand men, with the necessary
equipment, could be more easily obtained in the
Old World, and with the influence of the Spanish
Court, than at Panamá. He seems to have acted
in this matter with much circumspection and
secrecy. Instead of letting Almagro go alone,
or even accompany him, he takes the matter into
his own hands. His partner, the worthy school-

master, saw into his designs, and is reported to have said to Pizarro and Almagro, " Please God, my children, that you do not steal the blessing one from the other, as Jacob did from Esau; but I would that you had both gone together." It was a very apt illustration in character at any rate; for Pizarro was not unlike Jacob, and Almagro was the open-handed, plain, unsuspecting soldier of fortune.

Pizarro arrived safely in Spain, but had not long disembarked before that persistent Bachiller of law, Enciso, put him in prison, probably for some claim which he had against him in reference to the expedition of Ojeda. Pizarro was soon freed from this degrading imprisonment, and making his way to the Spanish Court, was well received there. His main object was speedily accomplished. He was confirmed in the rights of his discovery, and the government of Peru was assigned to him, the extent being defined to be two hundred leagues down the coast, from. Tenumpuela (the island of Puña is meant, I think) to Chincha; the title of Adelantado was also given to him; and the bishopric of Tumbez was assigned to Fernando de Luque. Pizarro then went to visit his native town Truxillo, in Estremadura. It is not often that a man has come back to his home with more renown; and he seems to have had the unusual fortune of inspiring his nearest relatives with some belief in him, or at least in his success. His brothers, Fernando (who was the only legitimate one), Juan, Gonzalo, and Martin, resolved to sell their estates and to join their brother Francisco in his enterprise. This gathering of the family around him apparently strengthened him much. His brother Fernando was a man of great ability, though of a nature and temperament which afterwards proved very detrimental to the governor.

Notwithstanding all these present advantages, Pizarro found it difficult to furnish the necessary complement of men for his vessels; and it was only by a trick that he contrived to elude the investigation of the king's officers at Seville, who had orders to see that his vessels were duly furnished and equipped, before being allowed to depart. One hundred and twenty-five men were all that he could number when he arrived at Nombre de Dios, from which port he made his way to Panamá.   The meeting of the principal partners was not at all friendly, for Almagro was naturally much discontented at the neglect, which Pizarro had shown of his interests at Court.   Hitherto the only fruits of Almagro's enterprise had been the loss of his eye, and the various debts which he had rendered himself accountable for;   and now he was not to share any of his partner's honours.   It may here be mentioned that Pizarro, in addition to other marks of favour which he had received, had been appointed a knight of the Order of Santiago.*   The arrival moreover, of Pizarro's brothers was not a pleasing circumstance to Almagro; and then began those feuds between him and the Pizarros, which afterwards led to the most deadly consequences.

By the advice, however, of common friends, the two associates were brought to terms; Pizarro agreeing to renounce the appointment of Adelantado in favour of Almagro, and binding himself not to ask any favour from the Spanish Court

---

* It is pleasing to find that the brave men who had stood by Pizarro in the Island of Gallo were made *hidalgos.*

for himself or his brothers, until he should have obtained a government for his partner, to commence where the limits of his own ended.

The preparations for departure were then completed, and Pizarro set sail from Panamá on the 28th of December 1530 in three small ships, carrying one hundred and eighty-three men and thirty-seven horses. Three years had already elapsed since he had returned from having discovered Peru, three long years no doubt to him, full, too, of disappointments and hindrances. He was obliged to set out also with a force far below what he considered necessary. This time, however, he reached the bay of San Mateo in three days, a distance which had before taken him two years and more. But now he found the people everywhere in arms against him. He seized upon the town of Coaque and captured booty to the amount of 15,000 *pesos* in gold, 1500 marks in silver and many emeralds. Upon this he sent his vessels back with the spoil to Panamá, hoping that they would soon return with men and horses. But the same misfortunes came down upon him now as upon his previous voyage, when he was obliged to wait for supplies, and his vessels had been sent away. It was several months before these vessels returned, and during that time Pizarro and his men underwent all the miseries of a most malignant climate. It may be that there was some compensation in all this waiting; for at this very time, as the Spaniards were wasting away by units, their future adversaries, the Peruvians, were busy in destroying their thousands by a civil warfare carried to the extreme of barbarous hostility.

After seven weary months the two vessels which had been sent to Panamá hove in sight, bringing twenty-six horse-soldiers and thirty foot-soldiers; and for these they had been obliged to endure all the miseries of the last seven months.

Pizarro then marched along the coast until he came opposite to the island of Puña. He and his men passed over in rafts to that island. There he was received with great apparent joy, to the sound of musical instruments; and the chief Curaca (cacique) gave him a sum of gold and silver. As it was the rainy season Pizarro resolved to take up his quarters there.

The inhabitants of Puña, however, not liking the continued proximity of such neighbours, planned an attack upon them. It was discovered by means of the interpreters, and the Curaca and his sons were immediately seized by Pizarro. This did not, however, prevent the attack; but the Indians were, after a contest of some hours, routed with great loss of life.

The Spanish commander then resolved to leave the island and to steer for Tumbez. By means of rafts which he compelled the Curaca to provide, he attempted to get his baggage across to the main land, putting a man in charge of each of the three rafts, while he and the rest of his men crossed over in the vessels and got safely to Tumbez. But the disposition of the natives here also was changed. Pizarro found the whole population in arms; they had intercepted his baggage and cut off the men in charge of it.

One ground for the change of disposition may be easily assigned. They were very different things, showing courtesy and hospitality to a few men in a boat, and receiving amicably a small armament in three vessels.

The Spanish commander demanded the production of his three men. Being set at defiance by the Indians, who were emboldened by having a river between them and the Spaniards, he caused a raft to be constructed, crossed over, routed them, and reduced the country to submission.

Pizarro now resolved to quit Tumbez and to found a town lower down the coast southwards. He accordingly took his departure on the 18th of May, 1532. After journeying for several days he selected a spot for his new town, which he called San Miguel. It was founded with all the usual formalities. Spanish residents were assigned to it, among whom the neighbouring Indians were distributed.*

Meanwhile vessels had arrived from Panamá with supplies, but with no troops; for Almagro, it was said, intended to come and colonize on his own account.

Pizarro, hearing this, wrote to Almagro when he sent the vessels back, begging him to change his project, and stating how much the service of God and his majesty would suffer from the establishment of another colony, as tending to frustrate the main design of the enterprise.

---

* This *repartimiento* was given conditionally.

It may here be observed how greatly the enterprise of Pizarro was facilitated by the establishment of the Spaniards at Panamá. There is no doubt that he suffered much, and was kept back owing to the scantiness of his supplies of provisions and men, yet what he accomplished would have been impossible unless there had been a source of recruiting at Panamá.

Pizarro, too, was fortunate in that he had not to contend against any tribes of Indians who made use of poisoned arrows. This alone was as good for him as if his armament had been quadrupled in number.

While Pizarro was at his new town he learned something of the country he was about to conquer. He heard that, on the road to places called Chincha and Cusco, there were populous towns very large and rich; and that a journey of twelve or fifteen days from San Miguel would bring him to a well-peopled valley, called Cassamarca, where Atahuallpa, the greatest monarch of those parts, was stationed. This prince had just come as a conqueror from a far-off land—his country, and having arrived at the province of Cassamarca (" cassa," hail, and " marca," a province), he had fixed himself there, because he had found it pleasant and rich, and from thence he was about to extend his conquests. Fernando Pizarro thus states in a letter his brother's knowledge at this time of the affairs of the Peruvian kingdom:—

" He heard that there was at Cassamarca, Atahuallpa, son of old Cusco, and brother of him who was at that time lord of the country. Between the two brothers there had been a very bloody war, and this Atahuallpa had gone on conquering the country as far as Cassamarca."

To use Cusco for the name of the reigning sovereign and that of his predecessor is much the same thing as if an invading army of barbarians, entering England, were to speak of the deceased and the reigning monarch as old and young London.

The ignorance, however, of the Spaniards about Peru was more than equalled by the ignorance of the Peruvians about the Spaniards. Indeed, the two great centres of American civilization were entirely dissociated. Nothing was known in Mexico of Peru: nothing in Peru of Mexico. The fall of Mexico had spread dismay far and wide in Central America, but not a rumour reached the golden chambers of the reigning Inca.   Yet a small and narrow strip of territory was all that intervened to check communication between the two great empires.

Had " old Cusco," or " young Cusco," been aware of the proceedings of the Spaniards either in Darien or at Mexico, a very different reception would have awaited them in Peru; but the conquest of America was commenced at a period when nations had been formed in that continent, but when international relations had been hardly at all developed.

CHAPTER IV.

ABOUT forty years previous to Pizarro's landing, Huayna Capac, the reigning Inca, went out from Cusco northwards to the province of Quito; and, conquering it, annexed it to the crown of Peru. By the daughter of the lord of Quito he had a son called Atahuallpa (" *Atahu*," virtue, in the Latin sense of valour, and " *allpa*," sweet). It is probable that in consequence of this conquest, he caused a great road which was afterwards the wonder of the Spaniards, to be made from Cusco to Quito, or rather, to be prolonged to Quito, from some intermediate point between the two cities. If so, this renowned Inca, both by his conquest and his road-

making, must have greatly facilitated the destruction
of his royal race.   Such are the triumphs of men!
This road must have been worked at when Columbus was finding his way from Spain to the West
India Islands, so that, in more ways than one, the
path was being smoothed for the hardy Asturian
or Biscayan, who had seldom seen anything more
valuable than dirty little adulterated bits of silver,
to the golden-plated temples of the Sun.   Happily men move about, for the most part, in a sort
of mist which allows them dimly to apprehend
the present, but which infuses itself between their
dull eyes and the future as completely as if it
were the most impenetrable thing in nature.   And
so Huayna Capac, the boasted descendant of the
Sun, heir to so much wisdom, little thought what
mischief to his country he had unwittingly been
the cause of, when, just before his death, he heard
of the advent of a few strange-looking, bearded
men, who had landed at a remote part of his dominions,—for, doubtless, he did hear of that
apparition of Pedro de Candia at the palace and
temple of Tumbez.   This intelligence, however,
probably filled the Inca with strange fears and
misgivings; and some expressions of his may be

the origin of those reports mentioned in the Spanish historians, that the Peruvians themselves had already forecast the fate of their dynasty. That dynasty was now a kingdom divided against itself. Huayna Capac was dead, and between his sons an internecine war was raging when Pizarro landed, for the second time, at Tumbez.

Atahuallpa, as before said, was the son of Huayna Capac, by the daughter of the conquered lord of Quito; but he was considered illegitimate —not in our modern and narrow sense of the word,—but simply that, not having a mother of the imperial race, he could not succeed to the throne of the Incas. Huayna Capac had other children who were legitimate, and of whom Guascar Inca (so called, as some say, from a golden chain* of immense size which was used at the dances given in honour of his birth) was the eldest, and therefore of right succeeded to the throne of Cusco.

Atahuallpa is said to have been a favourite of his father; he succeeded in gaining the affections of some of the late Inca's generals; and, after his father's death, whether by right, by fraud, or by

----

* " Huasca " means, in Quichuan, a rope.

force, he established himself upon the throne of Quito. The story then becomes very tangled, and is told in different ways. The main facts, however, are simply these:—that there were two brothers, both of them despots, dividing an inheritance, and the usual result in such cases took place in this. Guascar Inca, no doubt, beheld with concern the occupation of Quito by his brother, and regretted the division of a kingdom which had been ruled over by one supreme Inca. On the other hand, Atahuallpa doubtless considered himself as the legitimate sovereign of Quito, in right of his mother's claims, and would naturally be unwilling to render homage to Guascar Inca. War ensued between the brothers; and, while Pizarro was founding the town of San Miguel, Atahuallpa, by means of his generals, Quizquiz and Chilicuchima, had invaded Guascar's territories, taken Cusco, and made Guascar himself a prisoner. Quizquiz had exercised the utmost barbarities upon the royal race of Cusco, whom, though very numerous, he had nearly succeeded in exterminating; and, with Guascar himself as prisoner, the victorious general was returning from the South to rejoin his master,

Atahuallpa, in Cassamarca, at the very time when the Spaniards were descending from the North, and making their way to meet Atahuallpa in that beautiful valley. The dates of this transaction are a little dubious, but I assume that Atahuallpa's troops had already gained this victory; and I am strengthened in that assumption by the fact that Atahuallpa, when first seen by the Spaniards, wore the tasselled diadem which belonged to the Incas alone.

But the end of the Incas had arrived. Pizarro, with whose name Peru is now for ever hereafter to be connected, left San Miguel on the 24th of September, 1532, and commenced his march on Cassamarca; conquering or pacifying the Indian tribes that came in his way, and obtaining what information he could of the movements and designs of Atahuallpa. When the Spaniards had proceeded about half-way between San Miguel and Cassamarca, messengers from Atahuallpa presented themselves before Pizarro. Their message was friendly. They brought a present for the Spanish commander and some provisions for his men. The principal part of the present was a singular drinking-vessel, fashioned of some precious stone, in the form of a double castle. They said that their master was awaiting Pizarro at Cassamarca, and they mentioned that Atahuallpa's generals had been victorious. Pizarro replied with courtesy, and even made an offer of his services, to subdue Atahuallpa's enemies. Journeying on for two days, and resting each night in buildings that were fortified and surrounded with walls of dried mud, Pizarro arrived at a river which he forded. It was here that the Spaniards first learnt the way in which the Peruvians were numbered by tens and multiples of ten; and that five tens of thousands was the number of which Atahuallpa's army consisted. Proceeding onwards, Pizarro then came to the territory of a Curaca, named Cinto. Thence he despatched the Curaca of San Miguel as his envoy, to ascertain what were Atahuallpa's intentions, and whether any troops occupied the mountains between this point and Cassamarca. Pizarro was now upon one of the great roads between Cusco and Quito, and therefore each night he was enabled to rest in some one of the fortified places, at which the Incas themselves had been accustomed to stop. But, in the course of the next three days, Pizarro diverged from the main road, leaving it to the right, and prepared to ascend the mountain road, which led direct to Cassamarca. Atahuallpa seems to have been no great general, or to have had the fullest confidence in his own superiority of numbers and the pacific intentions of the Spanish commander, for he left unguarded this mountain pass, which a few men might have maintained against an army, the only road being so precipitous that, as Pizarro's secretary mentions, it was like the steps of a staircase. Arrived at the top of this mountain Pizarro again encountered messengers from Atahuallpa. Previously, however, to seeing them, the Spanish commander had received information from his own envoy that the ways were clear. This news was confirmed by the message from Atahuallpa, which was merely a request to know on what day Pizarro would arrive, in order that the Inca might make arrangements for supplying the Spaniards, in the course of their march, with food at the stations where they were to halt.

The new envoys from Atahuallpa recounted the story of the war between the brothers. They

said that Huayna Capac had left the principality
of Quito to their master; that Guascar Inca had
been the first to make war upon his brother; and
they confirmed the important news of Guascar's
capture.   Pizarro expressed his satisfaction at
Atahuallpa's success; and, in a commonplace way,
moralized upon the fate of ambitious men. " It
happens to them," he said, "as it has happened
to Cusco (he meant Guascar Inca): not only do
they not attain what they wickedly aim at, but
they also lose their own goods and their own
persons." The Spanish commander added this
formidable intimation from himself. He knew,
he said, that Atahuallpa was a puissant monarch,
and a great warrior; but his own master, the
King of Spain, was sovereign of the entire world,
and had a number of servants who were greater
princes than Atahuallpa. His King's generals,
indeed, had conquered kings more powerful than
either Atahuallpa or Cusco, or their former sovereign and father. Pizarro then proceeded to
account for his own presence there, saying that
the Emperor had sent him into that country to
bring its inhabitants to the knowledge of God;
and that, with the few Christians who accom-

panied him, he had already vanquished greater kings than Atahuallpa. The Spanish commander concluded by putting before the messengers an alternative. " If," he said, " Atahuallpa wishes to be my friend, and to receive me as such, in the way that other princes have done, I will be his friend. I will aid him in his conquest, and he shall remain on his throne (*i se quedará en su Estado*), for I am going to traverse this country until I reach the other sea. If, on the other hand, he wishes for war, I will wage it against him, as I have against the Curaca of Santiago (this was the name the Spaniards gave to the island of Puña), the Curaca of Tumbez, and all those who have chosen to make war upon me; but I shall not make war with any one, or do harm to any one who does not bring it upon himself." This speech, which perhaps may have been a little dressed up for the eyes of Charles the Fifth and his Court, was still, I dare say, substantially, what Pizarro uttered; as his policy certainly was to create terror. The Indian messengers listened in silence. afterwards they desired to report these things to their master; and Pizarro gave them leave to depart.

The next day Pizarro resumed his march, and in the evening the envoy whom Atahuallpa had first sent,—a man of importance, the same who had brought the present of the castellated vase,—presented himself in the Spanish camp. He, too, brought flattering assurances from Atahuallpa, declaring that that prince would treat Pizarro as a friend and brother. This Peruvian chief said that he would accompany Pizarro to Cassamarca.

Pizarro resumed his march, and the day after, Pizarro's own Indian messenger, the Curaca of the province of San Miguel, returned to the camp. No sooner did this Indian set eyes upon Atahuallpa's envoy, than he fell furiously upon him, and, if they had not been separated, would have done him serious injury. Being asked the cause of his rage, he said that this envoy was a great rascal, a spy of Atahuallpa's, who came there to tell lies and to pass himself off for a chief; that Atahuallpa had a numerous army with him, well-armed and well-provisioned; that he was preparing for war in the plain of Cassamarca; and that the town of Cassamarca was abandoned. The San Miguelite Indian's dignity had been deeply injured. They would not, he said, allow him to see Atahuallpa; they would not furnish him with provisions unless he gave something for them in exchange; indeed, he declared, they would have killed him, if he had not threatened that Pizarro would do the like with Atahuallpa's messengers. One, however, of Atahuallpa's uncles he had seen, and to him he had given an account of the bravery of the Spaniards, of their armour, their horses, their swords, their guns, and their cannon.

To these furious words Atahuallpa's envoy replied, that, if the town of Cassamarca was deserted, it was in order that the houses might be left vacant as quarters for the Spaniards; and that Atahuallpa was in the field, because such had been his custom since the commencement of the war. "If," he said, " they prevented you from speaking to Atahuallpa, it is because he is keeping a fast,* and, while he fasts, he lives in retreat. His people dare not then speak to him, and nobody

---

* It is a curious fact that several of the princes of Cassamarca, whom the Incas dispossessed, are said to have fasted to such a degree, upon first coming to the throne, as to have seriously injured their health. The shortness of their reigns is thus accounted for.—See BALBOA, p. 95; TERNAUX-COMPANS, vol. iv.

ventured to let him know that you were there.
If he had known of your arrival, he would have
received you, and would have given you to eat."
In addition to these assurances, Atahuallpa's envoy was ready with a great many arguments to
prove his master's good intentions,—so many,
indeed, that Pizarro's secretary, himself a man
delighting in brevity of speech, observes that if
all the discourse between Pizarro and the envoy
had been written down it would make a book.
The result was, that Pizarro pretended to be satisfied, and reproved his own envoy for his violence;
but, in reality, the Spanish commander continued
to entertain the gravest suspicions of Atahuallpa's
good faith.

The following day, Pizarro recommenced his
march, and passed the night on a savannah, where,
according to promise, Atahuallpa's messengers
brought provisions to the camp. On the next
day, Pizarro having divided his army into three
corps, proceeded towards the town of Cassamarca,
with the intention of taking up his quarters there
that night. As he approached the town he could
see Atahuallpa's camp, which lay upon the skirt
of a mountain, at the distance of one league.

It was on a Friday, the 15th of November, 1532, at the hour of vespers, that Pizarro entered Cassamarca. Close to the entrance there was a large square surrounded by walls and houses. I conjecture this to have been originally a *tambo* (i. e. a resting-place for the Inca in his journeys), for such must often have been the nucleus for a town. The first thought of Pizarro was to despatch a messenger to Atahuallpa, to let the Inca know of his arrival, and to ask him to come and assign quarters to the Spaniards. Pizarro's next thought was to examine the town, in order to see whether there was any stronger position for his troops to occupy than the great square. Meanwhile, he ordered that all his men should remain where they were, and that the horsemen should not dismount, until they knew whether Atahuallpa was coming.

The description of Cassamarca is very interesting, and the more so, from its not having been a town of the first magnitude. Indeed, Pizarro's secretary says that it contained only two thousand inhabitants; but most people are very bad judges of what space the inhabitants of another country would occupy. Cassamarca was built at the foot of a sierra, upon a flat space extending for a league. Two rivers traversed the adjacent valley; and the town was approached by two bridges, under which these rivers ran. The great square, larger than any at that time in Spain, was connected with the streets by two gates. In front of this square, and incorporated with it, in the direction of the plain, was a fortress, built of stone. Stone stairs led up from the square to the fortress. On the other side of this fortress, there was a secret staircase and a sally-port, connecting the fortress with the open country.

Above the town, on the hill-side, " where the houses begin," there was another fortress, constructed on a rock, the greater part of it scarped. This hill-fortress, which was larger than the other, had a triple enclosure, of more extent than the great square; and the ascent to it was by a winding staircase. There was still another enclosed space between the hill-fortress and the heights of the sierra, which was surrounded by buildings where the women-servants attached to the palace had their residence.

Outside the town, there was a building surrounded by a court open to the air, but enclosed
by mud walls, and planted with trees. This was
the Temple of the Sun. There were also many
other temples within the town. The houses, which
formed, as I imagine, two sides of the great square,
were very large. The frontage of some of them
occupied no less than two hundred yards, and they
were surrounded by walls about eighteen feet high.
The walls were of good and solid masonry. The
roofs of the buildings were formed of straw and
wood. The interior of these houses was divided
into several blocks of building, each of these
blocks consisting of a suite of eight apartments,
and having a separate entrance. In the court-
yards were reservoirs of water, brought from
some distance in tubes. The town was commanded by the fortress on the hill, and compressed, as it were, between that fortress and
the great square, where the government buildings
probably were. This square, again, with its
smaller fortress, commanded the open country.
Cassamarca was, therefore, a very strong and
well-arranged place for the warfare of that day.
It was a remark made by the first conquerors

of Peru, that the inhabitants of the higher country were always much more civilized than the natives of the plains, so that Cassamarca was probably a favourable specimen of a Peruvian town.*

Pizarro, having surveyed the town, and being convinced that there was no better position for his troops than the great square, returned to them there. Then, seeing that it was growing late, he despatched Fernando de Soto with twenty horsemen to Atahuallpa's camp, to urge that prince to hasten his visit. Fernando de Soto was to avoid any conflict with the Indians, but was to make an effort to penetrate to the Inca's presence, and to

---

* It is much to be regretted that the conquerors were not good draughtsmen : how many words it takes to give a most inadequate description of what a few strokes of the pencil might easily and accurately have conveyed.

It is curious to notice how soon familiarity with a new country takes away the power of describing it. We may look in vain for a better account of any Peruvian town than this given by Xerez; and the first description of Mexican houses given by the conquerors, in the letter of the town-council of Vera Cruz to the Emperor Charles the Fifth has a freshness and distinctness in it scarcely to be found in any subsequent notices of the buildings in New Spain.

return with some answer. Meanwhile, Pizarro mounted the fortress, to reconnoitre what could be seen of the Indian encampment. While there, his brother Fernando, having just heard of the embassage to the camp, came to Pizarro and suggested to him, that, as they had only seventy horsemen, it was hardly prudent to send so many as he had done with Fernando de Soto. This was true; for twenty were not enough to defend themselves, and yet too many for the Spanish commander to run any risk of losing. Pizarro listened to his brother's advice, and ordered him to go with another twenty upon the same errand, in order to support the others.

When Fernando Pizarro reached the Indian camp, he found that De Soto had already obtained an audience. Atahuallpa was at the entrance of his tent, sitting on a small seat, surrounded by a number of his chiefs and women, who stood in his presence. He had on his head the remarkable head-dress* appropriated to the Incas—"a tassel

---

* Many authors have endeavoured to describe the remarkable head-dress of the Incas, but, of all the descriptions that have been given, that of Oviedo's seems to be the most precise. He says that, in place of a

of wool, which looked like silk, of a deep crimson colour, two hands in breadth, set on the head with

---

crown, the Inca wore a red tassel, of a colour as brilliant as the most beautiful crimson, made of wool as fine as the choicest silk. " This tassel (*borla*)," he adds, "is as broad as a hand, or more, and a span long, and at the top it is gathered up in the shape of the flat brush which is used for scrubbing cloth ; and below is a broad fringe, which hangs from the head to the eyes, upon the forehead, and this drags it (the *borla*) down, and keeps it in its place, and so it (the fringe) covers the eye-brows and part of the upper eye-lids, in such a way, that in order that the inca may be able to see at his pleasure, he has to raise the fringe (lit. the beard), or to put aside the tassel."—" *Y esta borla es tan ancha ó mas que una mano, é luenga como un xeme, é arriba resumida como talle de escobilla de limpiar ropa, é lo de abaxo ancho aquel flueco que pende de la cabeça hasta los ojos ençima de la frente, é la trae contínuamente puesta, é assí cubre las cejas é parte de los párpados altos; de forma que para poder ver el Ynga á su pluçer, ha de alçar la barba ó apartar la borla.*"

Las Casas makes the *borla* descend lower still :—" Le colgava sobre la frente hasta casi la nariz, la qual hechava él á un lado quando queria ver."—LAS CASAS, *Hist. Apolo-gética*, MS., cap. 253.

It is worthy of notice, that there is some resemblance between the *borla* of the Incas and the common head-dress of the valiant Araucans, a circumstance which may indicate the origin of the Peruvian Incas.

" Los Araucanos no usan turbantes ni sombreros, pero

descending fringes which brought it down to the eyes."* This head-dress, as Xerez remarks, made the Inca look more grave than he really was. He kept his eyes fixed on the ground, without moving them. Fernando de Soto, by means of an interpreter, conveyed Pizarro's message. The Inca made no reply. He did not even lift up his head to look at the Spaniard: but one of the principal men of the Court spoke for him. Fortunately for the sake of history, Fernando Pizarro arrived at this moment; and Atahuallpa, being informed that this was the Spanish commander's brother, and receiving the same message from him, deigned to lift up his eyes and to make some reply himself. He said that Mayçabilica, a curaca of his,

---

llevan en la cabeza una faxa de lana bordada, á manera del diadema que usaban los antiguos Soberanos. Esta se la levantan ó alzan un poco, en señal de cortesía, al tiempo de saludar, y quando van á la guerra la adornan de varias vistosas plumas."—MOLINA, *Compendio de la Historia Civil del Reyno de Chile*, lib. ii. cap. 1.

 * " Tenia en la frente una Borla de Lana, que parecia Seda, de color de Carmesí, de anchor de dos manos, asida de la cabeça con sus Cordones, que le bajaban hasta los ojos."—F. DE XEREZ. BARCIA, *Historiadores*, tom. iii. p. 196.

on the banks of the river Turicara (this was near the town of San Miguel), had informed him how the Spaniards had maltreated his curacas, and had put them in chains. Mayçabilica, he added, had sent him an iron collar. The same chieftain had, moreover, told him that the Spaniards were no great warriors, and that he had killed three of them and a horse. Notwithstanding, however, the injuries complained of, he, Atahuallpa, would go with pleasure to-morrow morning to see the Spanish commander, and would be a friend to the Spaniards.

Fernando Pizarro replied with all the haughtiness that was to be expected from a Spaniard on being told that his countrymen were not warriors. " I told him," he says, " that the people of San Miguel were as women (hens, there is a report, was the word that Fernando used),* that one horse was sufficient to subdue the whole country, and that when he should see us fight, he would learn what sort of people we were,—that the governor had much regard for him, and that, if

---

* " Siendo todos ellos unas gallinas."—F. DE XEREZ. BARCIA, *Historiadores*, tom. iii. p. 196.

he had any enemy whom he would point out to the governor, he would send to conquer that enemy." To this the Inca replied, that our days' journey from this place there were some very stubborn Indians whom he could make no way with, and that the Christians might go there to help his people. " I told him," such are the words of Fernando, " that the governor would send ten horsemen, who would suffice for the whole country,—that his Indians were only necessary to hunt out the fugitives. Upon this, Atahuallpa smiled, as a man who did not so much esteem us."

As the sun had now gone down, Fernando Pizarro expressed some impatience for an answer to be given to the governor's message. The monarch replied, as before, that Fernando should inform his brother that Atahuallpa would come next day, in the morning, to see him, and that Pizarro should lodge his men in three large halls (*tres salones grandes*), which there were in the great square of Cassamarca, the middle one being reserved for the general himself.

Meanwhile, as it had begun to rain and hail, Pizarro had already appointed quarters for his men in the apartments of the palace, but had placed the captain of artillery and his two guns in the fortress. Previously to this, a messenger had come from Atahuallpa, bearing an answer in reply to Pizarro's first message, to the effect that the Spanish commander might have his quarters where he pleased, except in the fortress.

Fernando Pizarro returned to his brother that evening, and gave an account of his embassy. All that night the Spaniards kept good watch, and early on the next morning (Saturday) messengers came from the Inca, to say that he would come in the evening. Among these messengers was that envoy of Atahuallpa's who had before had so much conversation with Pizarro; and he told him that his lord said, that, since the Spaniards had come armed to his camp, he should choose to come with arms too. Pizarro replied that Atahuallpa might come as he pleased.

On the return of these messengers, about mid-day, Atahuallpa broke up his camp, and moved to within half a quarter of a league of Cassamarca. He then sent another message to Pizarro, saying that he would come without arms, but with a number of people who would form his suite, as he was going to take up his quarters in the town;

and he indicated where those quarters would be, namely, " in the House of the Serpent," so called because in the interior of the house there was an image of a serpent in stone. Either on this occasion, or on that of the former embassage, Atahuallpa had made a request that one of the Spaniards should be sent to accompany him. According to Xerez this was refused; according to Fernando Pizarro, it was acceded to.

Pizarro now made his final preparations to receive Atahuallpa. He kept the cavalry in the quarters that had been appointed for them,—the horses being saddled and bridled, and the soldiers ready to mount at a moment's notice. The infantry he posted in those streets which, as before described, led into the great square. The artillery was in the fortress; and Pizarro ordered the captain of the artillery to bring his pieces to bear upon the Peruvian army, now in their tents under the town. Pizarro himself remained in his own lodgings. He kept twenty men with him, who were to help him to seize upon Atahuallpa, " if the Inca came with treacherous intent, as it appeared he was coming with such a large body of men." Fernando Pizarro makes a similar remark

M

with regard to the cavalry, for he says, "they were to be ready until it was seen what were Atahuallpa's intentions."

Evening, always the best friend of the Indians in their encounters with the Spaniards, was now coming on. In the great square of Cassamarca a single sentinel paced up and down; and, as he could see what was going on in the enemy's camp, gave notice from time to time of their movements. Pizarro visited his posts, and addressed encouraging words to his men. They would rather have fought in the open fields, if fighting there was to be; and it was well to prevent this feeling from growing into anything like discouragement. Pizarro told his soldiers to make fortresses of their hearts, since there were no others for them, nor other succour but that of God, who protects in the greatest dangers those who are engaged in His service. "Although there may be five hundred Indians to one Christian," said Pizarro, "show that courage which brave men are wont to display on such occasions, and expect that God will fight for you. At the moment of attack, throw yourselves upon the enemy with force and swiftness; and let the cavalry charge in such a manner that the horses do not jostle against each other."

That the evening was coming on was a circumstance which Pizarro did not at all like. Accordingly he sent a messenger to hasten the Inca's arrival, on the pretext that he was waiting for him to sit down to supper, and that he could not do so until the Inca should arrive. Atahuallpa, on receiving this message, prepared to enter the town. He came accompanied by five or six thousand men—" unarmed men," Fernando Pizarro says,—that is, without their lances; but beneath their cotton doublets they carried small clubs, slings, and bags of stones.

While the Peruvians were moving into the town—and the movement of an Inca was a slow and pompous affair,—what were the thoughts of the leaders on both sides, and what had been their intentions throughout? Probably we shall not err much in concluding that neither Pizarro nor Atahuallpa had made up their minds definitively as to what course they should take; and that a very slight circumstance might have changed the proceedings of this memorable evening. How often must the audacious capture of Montezuma by Cortes have been talked over at their watch-fires by Spanish captains and Spanish soldiers! It is, therefore, not surprising that Pizarro should have made preparations for enacting a similar feat, if it should seem necessary. He had told his band of foot-soldiers that they were to endeavour to seize the Inca alive; but at the same time he had ordered that his men should not quit their posts, even if they should see the enemy enter into the great square, until they had heard the discharge of artillery. Fernando Pizarro mentions that some of the messengers who had come in the course of the day had told the Indian women attached to the Spaniards that they had better fly, as the Inca was coming in the evening to destroy the Christians. This story may be doubted; but the numbers that accompanied Atahuallpa, and the general movement of the camp to a spot much nearer the town, were evident facts of a threatening character. Still, I imagine that Pizarro was really anxious to penetrate the Inca's intentions, and, if he had been quite sure of their being pacific, would have been contented to wait the course of events.

As for Atahuallpa's designs, they were, I conceive, still less definitively formed. He may well have imagined that this small band of men might aid him greatly in completing and securing his conquests, while their numbers would be too few to be dangerous to his dominion. Still, he may have had a very wise apprehension of what even a few men, aided by these strange animals (horses and dogs), and with these wonderful weapons, of which he had heard something, might be able to effect. Pizarro's secretary thinks that the clubs and the slings were proofs of hostile intention. The braver Fernando Pizarro considered that they were no arms. The Inca himself probably thought that in the arming of his retinue he had chosen the happy medium: his attendants were not defenceless, but they did not come as the men of war whom he had left in the plain below. As for the number that accompanied him, he was, doubtless, accustomed to be surrounded by large numbers, and might have thought that his numerous and grand retinue would impress upon the minds of these strangers a just sense of the power and dignity of the Monarch of Peru.

Whatever were the thoughts or the intentions of either party, the time had now arrived for expressing them in action. Atahuallpa's retinue passed over the bridges, and began to ascend into the great square. The mode of their procession seems to show that the Indians had no expectation of an immediate attack, or they would hardly have suffered their prince to come so prominently forward. There was, however, an advance-guard, not, as it would appear, in great force, and not better armed than with the clubs and slings before mentioned. These entered the great square first. As the advance-guard began to enter, a troop of three hundred Indians, clothed in a sort of chequered livery, made clean the way before the litter of Atahuallpa. After them came three corps of dancers and singers, then a number of Peruvians in golden armour, wearing crowns of gold and silver, in the midst of whom was borne along the Inca himself, in a litter adorned with parroquets' plumes of all colours, and plated with silver and gold. A number of chiefs carried this litter on their shoulders. There were two other litters, and two hammocks, which no doubt contained persons of the highest rank and dignity. After these came several columns of men, about whose arms or armour nothing is said; but it is mentioned that they also wore crowns of gold and silver. As each body of men advanced, they deployed to the right or the left; and Atahuallpa's litter was borne on towards the centre of the great square. He then ordered a halt to be made, and that his litter and the others should be continued to be held up.

An incident happened now which is worth noting, as it shows how differently the same thing may affect different people, according to the mode in which they may be disposed to look at it. Pizarro's secretary says, " The Indians kept entering the square: an Indian chief of the advance guard then mounted the fortress where the artillery was, and raised a lance twice, as if to give a signal." Fernando Pizarro, at the same period of the narrative, says, " Twelve or fifteen Indians mounted a little fortress which is there, and took possession of it, as it were, with a flag attached to a lance." This slight action admits, as every one must see, of being rendered in two very different ways: either it was a traitorous signal to the army below, or a point of ceremony. I hold, with Fernando Pizarro, to the latter rendering.

At this point of time, Pizarro asked Vicente de

Valverde, the priest of the expedition, whether he would go and speak to Atahuallpa with an interpreter. Father Vicente consented, and advanced towards the Inca, bearing a cross in one hand, and holding a breviary in the other. As the priest approached, Atahuallpa naturally inquired of those Indians who had already seen something of the Spaniards, having journeyed with them, and provided for the necessities of the army, of what condition and quality this man was. One of them replied, that this was " the captain and guide of talk ; " he meant to say, preacher—" the minister of the supreme God, Pachacamác, and his messenger : " the rest, he said, " are not as he is."

Meanwhile, father Vicente had advanced close to the litter of Atahuallpa, and, having made his obeisance, addressed the Inca in a discourse,which was divided into two parts, and was intended to be a brief summary of the whole theology of that time.

First came the doctrine of the Trinity, three in one ; then a history of Jesus Christ, how He died on a cross like unto that which he, the father, bore in his hands ;—how He rose from the dead, and ascended into heaven, leaving His apostles and their successors to bring men to a knowledge of Him and His law; then he declared how the Roman Pontiffs were the successors of St. Peter, and have the same supreme spiritual authority.

He then proceeded to the temporal part of his oration; and explained how the Pope, in order to bring these nations back to the true knowledge of God, had granted the conquest of these parts to Charles the Fifth of Spain, who had sent his captains; and they had brought to the true religion the great islands and the country of Mexico: an alliance of perpetual friendship was therefore to be made between His Majesty and His Highness of Peru. He then explained what this alliance meant. It was that Atahuallpa should pay tribute, renounce the administration of his kingdom, obey the Pope, believe in Jesus Christ, and give up idolatry. " If, with an obstinate mind, you endeavour to resist," said father Vicente in conclusion, " you may take it for very certain that God will permit that, as, anciently, Pharaoh and all his army perished in the Red Sea, so you and all your Indians will be destroyed by our arms."

This last sentence is a triumph of pedantry; the fulfilment of the prophecy, however, was near at hand; and father Vicente can hardly be acquitted of having had some share in accelerating it. There is one feature of this remarkable scene that deserves mention, and it is that the interpreter was Felipillo, a native of the island of Puña, or of the adjacent country. It need not be asked what his Spanish was; indeed, his Cuscan, if he attempted it, must have been almost equally deplorable.

Atahuallpa had no sooner heard the priest's discourse than, according to Garcilaso de la Vega, he gave a groan, and uttered the word " Atac," (alas!); but, stifling his passion, he commenced an oration in reply to that of Vicente. He drew a contrast between the messages of peace and brotherhood which had previously been sent him, and the present menaces of fire and sword. He could not understand the mutual relation of the Pope and Charles the Fifth,—how Charles needed the authority of the Pope; and then he went into the question of tribute; if he had to pay tribute to any one, it was to one of those illustrious personages who had preceded the mention of Charles the Fifth, the Pope, or one of those composing the Trinity; " but if," he said, " I owe nothing to these others, I owe less to Charles, who never was lord of these countries nor has seen them." He is made to conclude by saying that the Spaniards had more gods than the Peruvians, who only adored Pachacamác, as supreme God, and the Sun as his subordinate, and the Moon as the sister of the Sun.

There is one thing, however, which the Inca undoubtedly did. He asked for the book which father Vicente carried in his hand, and to which he had referred as bearing testimony to his wonderful assertions. The book was clasped. Atahuallpa took it in his hands, but could not open it. Father Vicente advanced to do so for him; but the Inca, doubtless considering this a sign of disrespect, struck him on the arm, and then, forcing the book open, turned over some of the leaves; after which he threw it five or six feet from him.

He then said he well knew what the Spaniards had done on their route, how they had maltreated his curacas and pillaged houses. Father Vicente offered excuses, saying that the Christians had not done these things, but that some Indians, without Pizarro's knowledge, were the persons in fault; and that the Spanish Commander had ordered restitution. To this the Inca replied, " I will not go hence, until you have given me all that you have taken from my land." He rose up in his litter, and spoke to his people, and there was a murmur amongst them, as if they were calling for their armed companions.

Father Vicente returned to the Governor and told him what had passed, that the Inca had thrown the book upon the ground, and that the posture of affairs admitted of no more delay,* by which, I suppose, he meant that negotiation was at an end, and that arms must now decide the question. Then Pizarro put on his cuirass, took his sword and his buckler, and sent to inform his brother. It had been concerted between them, that Fernando was to give the signal to the captain of artillery, and he did so now. The cannon were discharged, the trumpets sounded, the cavalry rushed out of their quarters, and Pizarro himself, followed but by four men, who alone of all the

---

* This is upon Fernando Pizarro's testimony, and the words which he attributed to the priest are, " Que ya no estaba la cosa en tiempo de esperar mas!"—See Fernando's Letter to the Audiencia, in QUINTANA.

twenty could hold their way with him, rushed straight to the litter of the Inca, whom he seized by the left hand, uttering at the same time the war-cry of Santiago, a name well known now in many a bloody battle-field in the New World. The Inca's litter being still held up aloft, Pizarro could not get at him to drag him out of it, until the Spaniards had killed a sufficient number of the bearers, when it fell, and Pizarro, in the *mêlée* round the fallen Prince, was slightly wounded in the hand. At last the person of the Inca was secured, but in a woful plight, such as, perhaps, no rebel's dream had ever dared to depict for the person of his god-descended sovereign. The guards and the curacas did not desert their master, but were slaughtered in heaps around him. The rest of the Peruvians fled like sheep, and by their weight breaking down the wall of the enclosure (which that day, as the saying went hereafter, was kinder to them than the Spaniards), fled into the open country towards their camp. The Indians there, however, made no better stand than their flying comrades, and unresisted slaughter was the order of the day.

Pizarro's little wound was the only injury

received by any Spaniard, but two thousand dead bodies of Indians remained in the square that night.

The Inca, whose clothes in the struggle had been pulled to pieces, was reclothed, and " consoled " by Pizarro (a strange comforter!), who told him not to be ashamed of being conquered by one who had done great things, and to congratulate himself on having fallen into such merciful hands. " If we have seized upon you and killed your people," said Pizarro, " it is because you came with a numerous army; it is because you have thrown on the ground the book which contains the word of God; so the Lord has permitted that your pride should be humbled, and that no Indian should have been able to wound a Christian."

Atahuallpa is said to have made a reply, in which, after the fashion of despots, he laid the blame upon his inferior officers, saying that Mayçabilica had misrepresented the Spaniards' prowess, and that he, the Inca, wished to come peaceably, but that his chiefs would not allow him to do so.

It is not likely, however, that much discourse

passed between Pizarro and his captive that evening. As it was now late, Pizarro ordered the recall to be sounded; and soon afterwards the Spaniards returned, having with them no less than three thousand prisoners. Pizarro asked if any Spaniards were wounded, and was informed that one horse only had received a slight injury. Upon this, he gave thanks to God, and after saying that the great action of this day, which he counted as a miracle, was to be attributed to His grace and favour, he ordered the troops to rest in their quarters, bidding them, however, keep a good watch, "for," said he, "although God has given us the victory, we must not cease to be upon our guard."

They then went to supper. Pizarro and Atahuallpa sat at the same table. Afterwards the Inca retired to his couch, placed in the chamber of his conqueror, where he remained unbound, being watched over only by the usual guard that attended the Governor. What a contrast to the obsequious multitude that had been wont to throng the precincts of the Inca's dwelling! and with what feelings must the conquered monarch have looked round him at the break of dawn, in the first few moments after waking —that point of time when all great calamities are most keenly apprehended,—and when, if he had slept at all, he discerned that his defeat was not a hideous dream, but that he lay there a captive to these few bearded men who surrounded him, and that the vast apparatus of attendance that he was accustomed to was wanting! Pizarro, however, had not been unmindful of aught that might soothe his captive's sufferings; and, on the preceding evening, had offered to Atahuallpa the services of those female attendants of his who had already been captured: it may be hoped the monarch found amongst them those, or at least the one much-loved, who could console (rare art in man or woman!) without reproaching.

The position of Atahuallpa was almost unique. It is not merely that he was at the same time a conqueror and a captive. That conjuncture of circumstances had happened several times before in the world's history; but then the conqueror had usually been made captive by some detach-ment, or at least by some ally, of the other side; whereas, Atahuallpa, victorious on his own ground, suddenly found himself a slave to some power, which, so far as its connexion with Peruvian affairs was concerned, might have descended from the clouds. His previous success must have deepened the dismay he felt at his present reverse, and have added greatly to the height of hope from which he had suddenly and precipitately fallen.

Whatever may have been the poignancy of the Inca's feelings, his dignity forbade any expression of it. He spoke with resignation, and even with cheerfulness, of his defeat. He said it was the way of war, to conquer and to be conquered; and, with a wise stoicism, he sought to comfort those chiefs and favourites who were admitted to see him, and whose lamentations, not restrained by regal dignity, were loud and fervid.

The historian may well imitate the reserve of the principal sufferer, and forbear to moralize more than *he* did upon an unparalleled instance of the mutability of fortune, which was no less rapid than complete—as rapid, indeed, as the skilful shifting of a scene. The battle, if battle it can be called, in which perhaps hardly any weapons were crossed, except by accident, lasted little more than half an hour, for the sun had already set when the action commenced. It was rightly said that the shades of night would prove the best defence for the Indians. The Spaniards remarked that the horses, which the evening before had scarcely been able to move on account of the cold which they had suffered in their journey over the mountains, galloped about on this day as if they had nothing the matter with them. All that the fiercest beasts of the forest have done is absolutely inappreciable, when compared with the evil of which that good-natured animal, the horse, has been the efficient instrument, since he was first tamed to the use of man. Atahuallpa afterwards mentioned that he had been told how the horses were unsaddled at night, which was another reason for his entertaining less fear of the Spaniards, and listening more to the mistaken notions of Mayçabilica.

Saddled or not saddled, however, in the wars between the Spaniards and the Indians, the horse did not play a subordinate part; the horse made the essential difference between the armies; and if, in the great square of Madrid, there had been raised some huge emblem in stone to commemorate the Spanish Conquest of the New World, an equine, not an equestrian, figure would appropriately have crowned the work. The arms and the armour might have remained the same on both sides. The ineffectual clubs and darts and lances might still have been arrayed against the sharp Biscayan sword and deadly arquebuss; the cotton doublet of Cusco against the steel corslet of Milan; but, without the horse, the victory would ultimately have been on the side of overpowering numbers. The Spaniards might have hewn into the Peruvian squadrons, making clear lanes of prostrate bodies. Those squadrons would have closed together again, and by mere weight would have compressed to death the little band of heroic Spaniards. In truth, had the horse been created in America, the conquest of the New World would not improbably have been reserved for that peculiar epoch of development in the European mind, when, as at present, mechanical power has in some degree superseded the horse; and it is a real superseding, for the new power is naturally measured by the units contained in it of the animal force which it represents and displaces.

CHAPTER V.

*Agreement for Atahuallpa's Ransom — Fernando Pizarro's
Journey to the Temple of Pachacamác—Messengers sent to
Cusco—Arrival of Almagro at the Camp of Cassamarca.*

EARLY the next morning after the capture of Atahuallpa, the Governor (from henceforth we may well call Pizarro the Governor, and on his furrowed forehead might have been placed the potent diadem of the Incas) sent out thirty horsemen to scour the plain, and to ransack the Inca's camp. At mid-day they returned, bringing with them ornaments and utensils of gold and silver, emeralds, men, women, and provisions. The gold in that excursion produced, when melted, about eighty thousand *pesos.*

There was one thing which the Spaniards noticed in this foray, and reported to Pizarro. They found several Indians lying dead in the camp, who had not been killed by Spaniards (they knew their own marks); and, when Pizarro asked for an explanation of this circumstance from the Inca, he replied, that he had ordered these men to be put to death, because they had shrunk back from the Spanish captain's horse. This Spanish captain was Fernando de Soto, who, in his interview on the preceding day, had indulged in sundry curvettings, to impress upon the Peruvians a just appreciation of the prowess of the horse. Such little traits—and there are several of them in Atahuallpa's (Sweet Valour's) conduct—tend to diminish the sympathy which we might otherwise have had for him. In truth, in this melancholy story it is difficult to find anybody whom the reader can sympathize much with. Fernando Pizarro is said to have behaved well to the natives, and at this period of the conquest he always makes a creditable appearance; but, to any one who knows what direful mischiefs he will hereafter give rise to, his name suggests the ideas of discord and confusion.

On the present occasion, the Governor showed some consideration and mercy. Many of his men wished him to kill the fighting men among their prisoners, but he would not consent to this. They had come, he said, to conquer these savages, and to instruct them in the Catholic faith; and it would not be fitting to imitate these cruel people in their cruelties. Those Peruvians, therefore, whom the Spaniards did not choose for slaves were set at liberty.

Pizarro renewed with Atahuallpa the preaching of the previous evening. His discourse was probably more intelligible than that of the priest, Vicente de Valverde, of whom the earliest traveller (not a Spaniard) in those parts slily observes, when describing the interview between the priest and the Inca, that Valverde must have supposed Atahuallpa to have suddenly come out as some great theologian.* Pizarro, besides explaining matters of faith, instructed the Inca in political affairs, informing him how all the lands of Peru and the "rest (of the New World) belonged to the Emperor, Charles the Fifth, whom Atahuallpa must henceforth recognize as his superior lord." The

---

* "Ratus fortasse Attabalibam repenté in magnum aliquem theologum evasisse."—BENZONI, *Hist. Nov. Orbis,* lib. iii. cap. iii. p. 280.

dispirited Inca replied that he was content to do so; and, seeing that the Christians collected gold, he said that what they had hitherto got was little, but that for his ransom he would fill the room where they then were, up to a certain white line which he marked upon the wall, and which was about half as high again as a man's height, between eight and nine feet. This ransom was to be paid in about two months.

Pizarro did not fail to make many inquiries of Atahuallpa about the state of his dominions, and the war between his brother and himself. The Inca told him that his generals were occupying the great town of Cusco, and that Guascar Inca was being brought to him as a prisoner. It was an oversight in Pizarro, and one which Cortez, Vasco Nuñez, or Charles the Fifth would never have committed, that the Spanish Governor did not send at once to secure the person of the deposed Inca.* It must not be supposed, however, that the Spanish commander remained idle after

---

* If, however, Xerez is accurate, Guascar must have been put to death very soon after Atahuallpa's capture, and Pizarro at once informed of the fact.

his capture of Atahuallpa. He founded a church; he raised and strengthened the fortifications of Cassamarca; and he endeavoured to ascertain what were the movements and intentions of the Peruvians. Still, it was not to secure the person of Guascar Inca—and we must therefore conclude his fate to have been settled before then,—but to make sure of the promised gold (which metal soon was to become so plentiful that the Spaniards would shoe their horses with it), that the Governor determined to send his brother Fernando, after two months had passed, to collect the remainder of the ransom, and also to observe the Peruvian armies which were said to be approaching Cassamarca. Before this, the Governor had sent to his town of San Miguel, to inform them there of his successes; and on the 20th of December, he received a letter from that town telling him of the arrival, at a port called Concibi, near Coaque, of six vessels, containing a hundred and sixty Spaniards and eighty-four horses. The three largest of these vessels, with a hundred and twenty men, were armed and commanded by Pizarro's partner, Diego de Almagro; and the other three were caravels with thirty volunteers from Nicaragua. The Governor wrote to welcome Almagro, and to beg him to come on to Cassamarca.

Meanwhile, continually, messengers and men of great authority kept arriving to see their master Atahuallpa. Amongst others came the chief of the town of Pachacamác, and the guardian of the great temple there. The latter was put in chains by Atahuallpa, who, according to the Spaniards, seems to have become quite a recreant from his own religion, for he is made to say that he did this because the guardian of the temple had advised him to make war upon the Christians, and had declared that the idol had said to him that the Inca would kill them all. "I wish to see," the Inca is reported to say, "if he, whom you call your God, will take this chain off you." What is more certain is, that Atahuallpa, who was a man of much intelligence, made rapid progress in learning how to play chess and games with dice,—a part of the mission of the Spaniards which was sure to find a ready acceptance from the Indians.

It was on the day of the Epiphany, 1533, that Fernando Pizarro set off from Cassamarca with twenty horsemen and some arquebusiers. There is a minute account of his journey written by the King's *Veedór*, who accompanied him ; and Fernando himself has also given a short account of it. Everywhere they found signs of riches and of civilization. On his route Fernando obtained leave from the Governor to go to the city of Pachacamác, where was a great temple ; in reaching which he had to journey along the great roads. "The road of the Sierras," he observes, "is a thing to see, for, in truth, in a land so rugged, there have not been seen in Christendom such beautiful ways, the greater part being causeway."

On Sunday, the 30th of January, after traversing for some miles a country abounding in groves and populous villages, Fernando Pizarro reached Pachacamác, where he was well received by the inhabitants. He there entered the temple, which he found to be very dark and dirty. The presence of a Pizarro in the inmost recesses of that sacred fane was of itself the sternest blow to all that was idolatrous in the ancient religion of Peru.

While Fernando Pizarro was at Pachacamác, he heard that Atahuallpa's principal captain was at a town twenty leagues distant, called Xauxa. The name of this chief was Chilicuchima. Fernando put himself into communication with the Peruvian general, and, after much hesitation on his part, succeeded in persuading him to return with him to Cassamarca, which they reached on the 25th of March, 1533. Fernando Pizarro brought back with him twenty-seven loads (*cargas*) of gold and two thousand marks of silver.

The manner of Chilicuchima's approach to the presence of his sovereign excited the general remark of the Spaniards. As the Indian chief entered the town, he took from one of the Indians of his suite a moderate-sized burden, which he placed upon his shoulders. The rest of the chiefs did the same; and, laden in this singular manner, they entered the presence of their sovereign. When there, Chilicuchima raised his hands to the sun, and returned thanks to it for having been permitted to see the Inca again. Approaching his sovereign with much tenderness and with tears, he kissed his face, his hands, and his feet. The other chiefs did the same. But Atahuallpa, much as he regarded his great captain—and there was no one, we are told, whom he loved more,—

did not deign to take any more notice of him than of the meanest Indian in the room. Such was the abject adoration which was paid by the Peruvians to their Incas.

Fernando Pizarro's mission was not the only one which the governor had sent out from Cassamarca. He had also, at Atahuallpa's request, it is said, despatched three messengers to Cusco to receive the promised treasure and to bring him a report of the country.* These three men were, I believe, common soldiers, or very little above that rank, and their names were Pedro Moguer, Francisco de Zarate, and Martin Bueno. Borne along in hammocks on the shoulders of subservient Indians, regaled and reverenced almost as deities, these three uncultured men reached the grand city of Cusco, where they behaved with the greatest insolence, avarice, and incontinence. It was a terrible humiliation for that ancient and royal city to endure; and the devout Peruvians might well have wondered that the sun could bear to look down upon the indignities committed in his sacred city by these rude strangers. Having

---

* Xerez says that they were to take formal possession of Cusco, and that a public notary accompanied them.

been first taken for gods, they soon showed themselves to be a scourge from the gods. The people of Cusco meditated revenge; but, their fears or their respect for Atahuallpa prevailing, they hastened, by satisfying the demands of these three Spaniards, to get rid of them. The inhabitants of the royal city must have remained shocked and troubled to their inmost souls, and the spell which might have attached this simple people to the Spaniards was broken.

Indeed, we may well consider the sufferings of the inhabitants of Cusco as having something peculiar in them, even for the Indies.

While such indignities were being perpetrated at Cusco, Almagro and his men had arrived at Cassamarca, and now the fruits of an ill-cemented partnership, like that between Pizarro and Almagro, began to show themselves again. Well might Sixtus the Fifth say, as he did once, when addressing the Venetian ambassadors, " He that has partners has masters"—alluding to his difficulties with the conclave of cardinals; and, if the learned and the discreet can hardly manage conjoint action, how much more difficult must it be with rude, unlettered soldiers, like Pizarro and Almagro.   Fernando Pizarro, the most distinguished member of the family, could never conceal his contempt and dislike for the uncouth-looking Almagro; and when Almagro arrived at the camp, the common dislike, which had been soothed down at Panamá, broke out again at Cassamarca.

Moreover, there was a serious cause, if not for contention, at least for jealousy on the part of the newly-arrived soldiers under Almagro's command, when contemplating the good fortune of the men who had come with Pizarro, amongst whom were to be divided the heaps of gold which were gradually filling the room where the line of measurement was marked for Atahuallpa's ransom.   Pizarro, perhaps with some view for the moment of getting rid of his brother, now resolved to melt the gold which had been accumulated, and to send Fernando with the king's fifth to Spain.   It amounted to one million three hundred and twenty-six thousand five hundred and thirty-nine *pesos** of pure metal.   A record

---

* A *peso* was equivalent to four shillings and eightpence farthing.

has been kept of the division of the spoil, from which it appears that the horse-soldier received, upon the average, eight thousand *pesos*, and the foot-soldier between three and four thousand. The name of Vicente de Valverde is not in the list, so that at least the vice of avarice cannot be imputed to him. Pizarro made over to Almagro a hundred thousand *pesos* as a compensation for the expenses which had been incurred in their partnership. To Almagro's soldiers twenty thousand *pesos* were awarded, which seems a very small sum indeed, and must have been totally inadequate to satisfy their cravings. The whole sum did not amount to that which was paid to any three of Pizarro's horsemen, and would by no means have compensated for the extravagant increase in prices which this influx of gold caused in the Spanish camp.*

---

* The common price for a horse was fifteen hundred *pesos*; a bottle of wine cost seventy *pesos*; a sheet of paper ten *pesos*; a head of garlic half a *peso*.—See XEREZ, p. 233.

The strangest result, however, of this influx of gold was that creditors shunned their debtors, and absolutely hid themselves to avoid being paid.—OVIEDO, *Hist. Gen. y Nat. de las Indias*, tom. iv. lib. xlvi. cap. 13.

CHAPTER VI.

Guascar Inca's Fate—Atahuallpa's Trial—Atahuallpa's Execution.

WHILE this wholesale spoliation of Peru was going on, it had fared ill with Guascar Inca, the legitimate sovereign of that kingdom. There is a story, unsupported by much evidence, but which appears not improbable, that Pizarro's messengers to Cusco met those persons who had charge of the fallen Inca, and that he implored the Spaniards to take him under their protection, and to convey him to Pizarro's camp, offering, as might be expected, great largesses. But they, not a whit more politic in this respect than their master, took no heed of his request, and passed on to Cusco. It is added that the fact of this interview being communicated to Atahuallpa hastened Guascar Inca's death. It is also said that Atahuallpa, fearing what Pizarro would say and do, if he gave the order for his brother's execution, made a trial of the Governor; and, on Pizarro's coming to visit him one day, he assumed a very sorrowful appearance. Being pressed to declare the cause of his grief, he said that Guascar Inca had been put to death by the captains who had charge of him, without his (Atahuallpa's) orders. Pizarro is said to have soothed him with some commonplace remark about death being the ordinary lot of mortals, whereupon the Inca no longer hesitated to give orders for his brother's execution.

The truth is, that the Scotch form of verdict, "not proven," is all that can be said against Atahuallpa, as regards his brother's death.

In a document, drawn up for Charles the Fifth's perusal, signed by the Governor, there is no mention of the death of Guascar Inca as part of the charge against Atahuallpa.

Atahuallpa seems to have been well aware that the newly-arrived Spaniards were anything but favourable to him. On taking leave of Fernando Pizarro, he said, " I am sorry that you are going; for when you are gone, I know that that fat man and that one-eyed man will contrive to kill me."

The fat man was Alonzo Riquelme, the King's treasurer; the one-eyed man was Almagro.

Then, too, it has been stated that the interpreter Felipillo, being in love with one of Atahuallpa's wives or concubines—an affront which, it is said, the Inca felt more than anything that had occurred to him,—was desirous of compassing Atahuallpa's death. It has been believed by some that Pizarro had from the first intended to put his prisoner to death; but this is probably one of those numerous instances of a practice indulged in by historians of attributing a long-conceived and deliberate policy to their heroes in reference to some event, because the event was all along familiar to the historian's mind, though not at all so to the mind of the hero of the story.

If I read Pizarro's character rightly, he may have been a suspicious man, but he was not a man of deep plans and projects. That he was likely to conceal his plans, when formed, is true; and there is a pleasing little anecdote indicative of his character in that respect, which may be mentioned here. Hearing that one of his soldiers had lost

his horse, and was unable, from poverty, to pur-
chase another, Pizarro concealed under his robe a
large plate of gold, and going down to play in the
tennis-court, where he expected to meet this soldier, but where he did not find him, the Governor
played on for hours, with this great weight about
him, until he espied the soldier and was able to
draw him aside and give him the gold in secret,
not without complaining of what he had had to
endure in playing tennis with such a burden
about him.   In addition, moreover, to his natural
cautiousness, it appears that Pizarro, in the course
of his long warfare with the Indians, had become
particularly wary in dealing with them.   In short,
he was a prudent soldier, but not a dissembling
statesman.   He may be acquitted of any deep-laid
design against Atahuallpa's life.   Far from being
the first to plot, it is probable that his hostility
was quickened or evoked by his fear of being out-
witted by the address of the Inca.

The truth is that Cassamarca, the present
scene of action, was in a country where the natives were not friendly to Atahuallpa: many of
them, therefore, would be glad to spread injurious
reports of the Inca's designs.   Moreover, in the

present condition of the Peruvian royal family, the Indians throughout the empire must have been in a very disturbed and uncertain state; and their movements, directed perhaps by private impulses, might present an appearance of warlike levies sanctioned by the Inca. Besides, it might naturally be expected that Atahuallpa's adherents, with or without his orders, would assemble together, and march towards the place of their master's imprisonment. Atahuallpa was therefore likely to suffer in the estimation of his captors by what was done by his friends, by his enemies, and by any bands of lawless men who were the enemies of the state.

The natural fears of men so isolated as were Pizarro and his Spaniards at Cassamarca would aid in bewildering their judgment as to the nature of any movements observed among the surrounding Indians.

Notwithstanding the immense superiority of the Spaniards in arms and accoutrements, it must not be forgotten that they were but a handful of men among the millions whom they had insulted, bereaved, and plundered; and that a dexterous surprise on the part of the Peruvians might easily restore the advantage to the side of numbers. There was, then, good reason for discussing what should be done with Atahuallpa; and the main body of Almagro's men were likely to take the side of the question unfavourable to the captive Inca, from a fear that whatever gold came in might be set down as a part of the ransom, on which Pizarro's men had the first claim, and also from a wish for some new adventure in which they, too, might distinguish and enrich themselves. The arrival, therefore, of Almagro and his men at this particular juncture must be accounted one of those inopportune contingencies with which the history of the conquest of America abounds. It gave occasion for a great difference of feeling upon the pending question of Atahuallpa's death: that question, once discussed, would be sure to become a subject for faction in the small community; and the rage of faction, like that of infectious disease, depends upon the smallness and confinement of the area over which it acts.

There is one circumstance which seems to have escaped the knowledge, or the observation, of the early chroniclers and historians, who all leave their readers in doubt whether Atahuallpa's ransom was ever fully paid. But in the narrative made for the Emperor, which may be considered as having an official character, and which bears the signature of Pizarro, there is the following passage. " That fusion (of gold) having been made, the Governor executed an act before a notary, in which he liberated the Cacique Atahuallpa and absolved him from the promise and word, which he had given to the Spaniards who captured him, of the room of gold which he had conceded to them; which act the Governor caused to be published openly by sound of trumpet in the great square of that city of Cassamarca." At the same time Pizarro caused the Inca to be informed that, until more Spaniards should arrive to secure the country, it was necessary for the service of the King of Spain that he should still be kept a prisoner. The reasons alleged for this apparent breach of faith were the greatness of Atahuallpa's power, and the fact, which Pizarro asserted he was well aware of, that the Inca had many times ordered his warriors to come and attack the Spaniards. It is difficult to see any motive for the singular proclamation mentioned above but a very prudent desire, on the part of Pizarro, to remove any cause of dispute between his men and those of Almagro in reference to the Inca's ransom. This proclamation, therefore, was an act in favour of Atahuallpa—that is, so far as the removal of the grounds on which a party is formed tends (which is but little for some time) to dissolve the party. That Pizarro had any personal regard for his captive may be doubted; and the common story of Atahuallpa's discovery that the Spanish commander could not read, and of his consequent contempt for him, though not perhaps literally true, may yet indicate that the relations between them were not those of particular friendliness.

Things being in this state, a circumstance occurred which Pizarro's secretary mentions, and which he says deserves to be mentioned. An Indian chief, the " Cacique " of Cassamarca (Cassamarca was one of the territories that had been conquered by Atahuallpa) came to the Governor, and by means of the interpreters informed him that Atahuallpa had sent to his own province of Quito, and to all the other provinces, to assemble men of war; that the army, thus formed, was marching under the command of a chief named Llaminabe; * that it was close at hand, and would arrive at night, when an attempt would be made to fire the town. The Cacique added other details. Pizarro expressed his warmest thanks for this intelligence, and ordered a notary to make a report of the matter, and to found an inquiry upon it. In consequence of this, an uncle of Atahuallpa's and several Indian chiefs were arrested and examined; and it was said that their evidence confirmed the evidence of the Cacique of Cassamarca.

The Governor then had an interview with the Inca; and, reproaching him for his treachery, told him what he had discovered. "You mock me," Atahuallpa replied, with a smile; "for you are always saying things of this absurd kind to me. What are we, I and my people? how can we conquer men so brave as you? Do not utter these jests to me." The Inca's smile and untroubled reply created no confidence in the mind of his hearer, for "since the Inca had been

* Ruminavi ("Stony-Countenance"), one of Atahuallpa's greatest captains.

a prisoner, he had often replied with such astuteness and composure, that the Spaniards who had
heard him were astonished to see so much address
in a barbarian."*

Pizarro sent at once for a chain, which he
ordered to be put round the Inca's neck—a
terrible indignity for the descendant of so many
monarchs to endure.　The Governor then took
a wiser step in despatching two Indian spies in
order to ascertain where this army was.　They
learnt, it is said, that it was advancing by little
and little through a mountainous part of the
country; that Atahuallpa had at first ordered it
to retreat; but that he had since countermanded
that order; and had now named the very hour
and place at which the attack was to be made,
saying that he should be put to death if they
delayed their arrival.　The Governor, upon this
intelligence, took all precautions against an immediate attack.　The rounds were made with the
greatest watchfulness; the soldiers slept in their
armour; the horses were kept ready saddled.　It
appears, also, that a party was sent out, under the

------

* See Xerez, p. 234.

command of Fernando de Soto, to reconnoitre; but the crisis of Atahuallpa's fate came on before any intelligence was received from them.

The camp being in this excited and watchful state, there came to it one Saturday morning at sunrise two Indians, who were in the service of the Spaniards, and who said that they had fled at the approach of an army which was only three leagues from Cassamarca, and that the Spaniards would be attacked that night, or the succeeding one.

Then Pizarro delayed no longer, but resolved to bring Atahuallpa to judgment, although, says the official narrative, it was very displeasing to the Governor to come to that pass. There happened to be a doctor of laws in the Spanish camp, and so the cause was conducted with due formality. The various counts in the indictment are given by Garcilaso de la Vega. Some of them are very absurd, but I should be reluctant on that account to pronounce that they are not genuine. Guascar Inca's death, as might be expected, formed one of the subjects for accusation; * and,

---

* This statement is not inconsistent with the fact of that

amongst other things, it was asked, whether Atahuallpa was not an idolater,—whether he had not prosecuted unjust wars,—whether he did not possess many concubines,—whether he had not made away with the tribute of the empire since the Spaniards had taken possession of it,—whether he had not made over to his relations and his captains many gifts from the royal estate since the arrival of the Spaniards; and, lastly, which was the gist of the matter, whether he had not concerted with his captains to rebel and to slay the Spaniards? If Felipillo did desire the Inca's death, now was the time when a word, put in or left out, might easily turn the scale. It seems that the prisoner was allowed to have an advocate; but little could be done by him for his client, if the two Indians, as interpreted by Felipillo, spoke decisively to the truth of their story.

The cause having been heard, and condemnation being resolved upon, judgment was pro-

---

part of the charge respecting Guascar Inca's death not being reported to the Emperor, for it may have been successfully rebutted.

nounced. It was to the following effect:—that Atahuallpa should be put to death, and that the mode of his death should be burning, unless he previously embraced the Christian faith. These raging missionaries, the Spanish conquerors, were always eager to put forward that part of their mission, which consisted in enforcing the outward acceptance of Christianity—a thing which, it must be admitted, they really believed to be of the utmost import.

When the sentence was communicated to the Inca, loud were his protestations against the injustice, the tyranny, and the ill-faith of Pizarro; but all these complaints availed him nothing; and he prepared himself for death with that dignity which men who have long held high station and have been accustomed to act before a large audience are wont to show—as if they said to themselves, " We play a great part in human life, and that part shall suffer no diminution of its dignity in our hands." When brought to the place of execution, he said that he would be a Christian— the threat of burning being found, as it often has been, a great enlightenment upon difficult points of doctrine. Vicente de Valverde baptized the

Inca under the name of Don Juan Atahuallpa, and the new convert was then tied to a stake. Just before his death he recommended to the Governor his little children, whom he desired to have near him; and with these last words, the Spaniards who were surrounding him being good enough to say the "Credo" for his soul, he was suddenly strangled with a cross-bow string. That night his body was left in the great square, and in the morning he was buried with all pomp and honour in the church which the Spaniards had already built, "from which mode of burial," adds the official document, "all the principal lords and caciques who served him received much satisfaction, considering the great honour which had been done to him, and knowing that by reason of his having been made a Christian he was not burnt alive, and that he was buried in the church as if he had been a Spaniard."

Atahuallpa, at the time of his death, was a man of fine presence, about thirty years of age, tending to corpulence, with a large, handsome, cruel-looking face, and with blood-shot eyes. His disposition was gay—not that his gaiety was manifested with his own people, for dignity forbade that, but in his conversation with the Spaniards. The general impression of his abilities seems to have been favourable, and he was supposed to be an astute, clever man. In short, had the tables been reversed, and Atahuallpa been born in Estremadura instead of in Quito, he would probably have made as crafty, bold, unscrupulous, and cruel a commander as any one of his conquerors; and, I doubt not, would have been equally devout. With his death fell the dynasty of the Incas, though afterwards, as we shall see, there were some mock-suns of Incas set up by the Spaniards, to serve their own purposes.

It is difficult to say whether the execution of Atahuallpa was politic or not. But certainly the whole scheme of Spanish conquest, as exemplified in Peru, was most unwise, if the preservation of the natives and their conversion are to be considered among the principal objects of the conquest, as they certainly were by many good men even at that early period. The conquest always proceeded too fast; and the want of sufficient opposition prevented a sound growth in the new Spanish states. The Spaniards found themselves suddenly masters—in one day masters—of vast tracts of country and populous nations, about whose laws, manners, government, religion, language, and resources they knew almost nothing. This was too difficult a problem for human nature to solve.   Accordingly, the conquerors spread themselves, or, to use a bold metaphor, were spilt, over the country they conquered, like some noxious chemical fluid which destroys all life it touches; and well, indeed, might they have been considered as the plague of an offended deity! No legislation could prevent the evil consequences of a state of things so entirely abhorrent from good government as this was.

There are, unfortunately, no more New Worlds to conquer; and human wisdom, which ever lingers on the road, and lives so much in retrospect, that a cynic would say it might almost as well deal with another world as so exclusively concern itself with the past history of this one, was certainly not more rapid or felicitous than usual in applying itself to the difficult circumstances which this newly-discovered continent produced in such abundance.   It has been intimated before, and the history of Peru confirms the remark, that a

weightier and more sustained endeavour on the
part of the Spaniards to conquer and colonize, or
mere missions to convert the natives, or simple
traffic like the beginnings of the British East
India Company, would probably have had a much
less unsuccessful issue in civilizing, converting,
and maintaining alive the inhabitants of the New
World. But it is not for any one generation to
comment very severely on its predecessors. The
history of the most advanced times presents nearly
as much that is ludicrous, disastrous, and ill-con-
sidered, as can readily be met with at any previous
period of the world.

Thus, with some regrets, and much foreboding,
we draw the curtain across the stage on which
lies the body of the last great Inca,—to be borne
by the Spaniards, with so much self-satisfaction
at their own piety, not to any golden-plated
temple of the sun, but to their hastily-raised
wooden church in Cassamarca. Meanwhile, in
the distance, there rises before the prophetic eye
a great picture, in which the lofty roads of Peru,
the sumptuous temples, palaces, and gardens are
already falling into swift destruction,—hencefor-
ward to possess the interest only of ruins, and to

be numbered with Babylon, Nineveh, and the things that have been.

Man is the great conservator; man the great destroyer: but the most fatal destruction—the destruction that continues to destroy—is when men stifle the inner life, and slay the spirit, of their fellow-men. The historian of the decline and fall of Rome has declared that it was not the barbarians who destroyed the buildings of " the eternal city," but the Roman citizens themselves, whose polity was broken up, who lived in a place too big for them, and who quarried amongst the grand edifices of their forefathers, to provide for their mean, daily purposes. So it is always; and no calamity is to be deeply apprehended for a people, which does not strike a mortal blow at the national life of that people. The direst earthquakes (and no quarter of the globe has suffered more from these appalling disasters than the New World,) leave but a slight scar behind. The most immense catastrophes of fire and flood, if the nation be but heartily alive, are soon smoothed over, and in a generation are not to be discerned, except by an increase of beauty in the city and of fertility in the fields. The most cruel wars often invigorate: Rome rises only greater from the vital conflicts she endured at the hands of the unrivalled Carthaginian. Nay, even conquest will not efface the essential being of a nation; and many a people, compressed into narrower limits, or absolutely subjugated by a dominant race, have bided their time, drinking in the secret benefits of great reverses,—have then raised their crests again, and become a world-famous nation.

But the Spanish Conquest, both of Peru and Mexico, was one of those fatal blows to the conquered, of which the shock runs through national and social life, smiting the spinal cord of a people, and leaving them in a death-like paralysis. The men in a nation so subdued are as helpless and bewildered as animals would be who had lost their instinct. All that the nation has accomplished in art, through science, or in architecture, is submissively ceded to the elements; and no man lifts his hand to protect or restore any work of his own or of his forefathers, which he had formerly delighted in. It is not an earthquake which has shaken these miserable men, but a new formation of their world that has overwhelmed them. All the old civilization—the record often of so much toil and blood and sorrow—is crushed for ever into a confused heap of rude materials, the simplest meaning of which it will hereafter require great study to decipher; and the nation, if it survives in name, is but a relic, a warning, and a sign,— like some burnt-out star, drifting along, hideous and purposeless, amidst the full and shining orbs which still remain to adorn and vivify the universe.

BOOK THE THIRD.

CHAPTER I.

*The Feud between the Pizarros and the Almagros—Alvarado's
Entrance into Peru—Almagro proceeds to conquer Chili—
Fernando Pizarro takes the Command at Cusco.*

WHEN the wild beasts of a forest have hunted down their prey, there comes the difficulty of tearing it into equal or rather into satisfying shares, which mostly ends in renewed bloodshed. Nor is the same stage of the proceedings less perilous to associates amongst the higher animals; and men, notwithstanding all their writings and agreements, rules, forms, and orders, are hardly restrained from flying at each others' throats, when they come to the distribution of profits, honours, or rewards. The feud between the Pizarros and the Almagros is one of the most memorable quarrels in the world. Pizarro and Almagro were two rude unlettered men, of questionable origin; but their disputes were of as much importance to mankind as almost any which occurred in that century, rich as it is in historical incident, except perhaps the long-continued quarrel between the Emperor Charles the Fifth and Francis the First. Moreover, the European feud between these monarchs was important chiefly on account of its indirect consequences, inasmuch as it gave room for the Reformation to grow and establish itself; but this dire contest in America destroyed almost every person of any note who came within its influence, desolated the country where it originated, prevented the growth of colonization, and changed for the worse the whole course of legislation for the Spanish colonies. Its effects were distinctly visible for a century afterwards, whereas the wars between France and Spain, though they seemed to be all-important at the time, did not leave any permanent mark upon either country.

There were no signs, however, of the depth and fatality of this feud between the Pizarros and the

Almagros at the period immediately succeeding
the execution of Atahuallpa. That act of injustice having been perpetrated, Pizarro gave the
royal *borla* to a brother of the late Inca, and set
out from Cassamarca on his way to Cusco. It
was now time to extend his conquests and to
make himself master of the chief city in Peru.
Accordingly, in company with his comrade Almagro and the new Inca, Pizarro quitted Cassamarca in the summer of 1533, having remained in
that beautiful district seven months.

It is unnecessary to give any detailed account
of the events of this journey. The hostile Indians, wherever met, were encountered and routed
by the Spaniards with the aid, as they imagined,
of their tutelary saint, whose assistance, however,
does not seem to have been much needed. The
newly-appointed Inca died. The death of this
prince has been attributed to the grief he felt at
the depression of his royal race. It is said that
after the *borla* had been placed upon him, he was
no sooner out of Pizarro's presence, than, tearing
the regal emblem from his forehead, he threw it on
the ground, and stamped upon it, declaring that
he would not wear a thing which he regarded as

a mark of his slavery and of his shame. His most devoted followers sought to conquer this resolution. But they did so in vain; and, giving way to unutterable disgust at his subservient position, he expired in two months' time after he had received the *borla* from the hands of the man who had conquered his people and taken away his brother's life. Pizarro exceedingly regretted the death of this Inca, for it was very convenient to the Spanish conqueror to have at his beck a scion of the royal race, who must be submissive to him, but whose semblance of authority might prevent the Peruvians from attempting further resistance.

Chilicuchima, the unfortunate general whom Ferdinand Pizarro had persuaded to accompany him to the Spanish quarters, became suspected of being in communication with the enemy, and was most unjustly condemned to be burnt by Pizarro. When the Spaniards approached the city of Cusco, they found that the Indians there were disposed to make a great resistance. But a brother of Guascar, named Manco Inca, who held the chief authority in the place, and was accounted by the Cuscans as the reigning Inca, came out to meet Pizarro as a friend, in consequence of which the Spaniards entered " the great and holy city " of Cusco after a slight resistance, on the 15th of November, 1533.*   Notwithstanding that Cusco had been rifled in the first instance by Pizarro's messengers, there still remained in that city great treasures, which, when divided into four hundred and eighty parts, gave, as some say, four thousand *pesos* to each Spaniard in the army.   Amongst the spoil were ten or twelve statues of female figures, made of fine gold, as large as life, and " as beautiful and well wrought as if they had been alive."   This division having been accomplished, Pizarro attended to the affairs of religion.   He caused the idols to be pulled down, placed crosses on all the high-ways, built a church, and then, with all due solemnities, in the presence of a notary and of fitting witnesses, took possession of the town in the name of the invincible King of Castille and Leon, Don Carlos the first of that name.

In the meantime, the fierce and valorous cap-

---

* This was exactly a year after their entry into Cassamarca, which had taken place on the 15th November, 1532.

tains of Atahuallpa did not remain indolent or pacific spectators of the Spanish conquest. But nothing would have availed, for the Spaniards were now ready to flock into Peru from all quarters.

One of the most renowned companions of Cortes, Pedro de Alvarado, was attracted by the report of the riches of Peru to try his fortune there.

The dismay of Pizarro may be imagined, when he heard that Alvarado, with no fewer than five hundred men at arms, had landed on the northern coast of Peru. He at once despatched Almagro in hot haste to conquer or to gain over this new and formidable rival. These new invaders, having met with great hardships, were not unwilling to come to terms with Almagro. Negotiations, therefore, were readily entered into, and a treaty agreed upon that Almagro should give to Alvarado one hundred thousand *pesos*, and in return Alvarado should hand over the armament to the two partners Pizarro and Almagro, and should engage for himself to quit Peru.

And now to effect the conquest of Peru the combined forces amounted to something very like what Comogre's son years before this had declared to be necessary.

It would seem at first sight that a great danger had been obviated in Alvarado's men having been thus brought into the service of Pizarro and Almagro; but it fell out otherwise, for the principal men in Alvarado's armament, having first met with Almagro, became attached to him, and were among his most zealous partisans; and partisanship brought ruin to every leader concerned in it, and was for years the curse of Peru.

Pizarro, relieved from his difficulty by the departure of Alvarado, resolved to found a city near the sea-coast, in the valley of Lima, which afterwards received the name of Lima. Before this occurred, however, the compact between the two partners, Pizarro and Almagro, had been renewed with oaths and other solemn affirmations; and it was agreed that Almagro should go to reside at Cusco, to govern that part of the country, for which Pizarro gave him powers, as he did also to make further discoveries southwards. The Mariscal (such was the title which had recently been conferred on Almagro) took his leave accompanied by the greater part of Alvarado's men, whom he had attracted by his amiable nature and profuse liberality.

While these events had been occurring in Peru, Fernando Pizarro had reached the court of Spain. It was in January, 1534, that he arrived at Seville, and as the Emperor was in Spain that year, Fernando Pizarro's business was readily despatched. The result of his negotiation with the court was, that he obtained for his brother the marquisate of Atavillos, a valley not far from Xauxa; the habit of Santiago for himself; the bishopric of Cusco for Vicente de Valverde; and a governorship for Almagro, which was to commence where Pizarro's ended, and was to be called Nueva Toledo. It cannot be said that Fernando Pizarro fell into the error formerly committed by his brother of neglecting Almagro's interests at the Spanish court. On the other hand, as some acknowledgment of these honours and dignities, Fernando held out hopes of procuring from Peru a large donation to the Emperor, who was about to commence his expedition to Barbary.

The tenour of the despatches, which were to confer these appointments, must have been known

to many persons; and while Pizarro was at Truxillo, another town which he founded on the coast,
a youth landed there who said that Diego de Almagro was appointed governor of the country
from Chincha southwards. Upon this, a certain
man named Aguero, anxious no doubt to secure
the present which it was customary to give on the
receipt of great good news, hastened after the
Mariscal, and found him at the bridge of Abançay,
where he communicated this intelligence to him.
It served to exalt Almagro greatly in his own
opinion. Some say that he threw up the office
which he held under Pizarro, claiming to rule
Cusco on his own account; others, that Pizarro
recalled the powers with which he had entrusted
Almagro for the government of Cusco, appointing
his brother Juan Pizarro to be governor. It is
certain that dissensions between the younger
Pizarros and Almagro arose at this time, which
the Marquis was obliged to come to Cusco to
pacify. Pizarro, on meeting his old friend, after
they had embraced with many tears, spoke thus:
" You have made me come by these roads without
bringing a bed or a tent, or other food than maize.
Where was your judgment, that, sharing with me

equally in what there is, you have entered into quarrels with my brothers?"   Almagro answered that there was no occasion for Pizarro to have come with all this haste, since he had sent him word of all that had passed; and, proceeding to justify himself, he added that Pizarro's brothers had not been able to conceal their jealousy, because the King had honoured him.

The licentiate Caldera, a grave and wise man, now intervened, as he had done before between the Mariscal and Pedro de Alvarado; and the result was that the Marquis and the Mariscal renewed their amity in the most solemn manner, standing before the altar, and each invoking upon himself perdition of soul, body, fame, honour, and estate, if he should break this solemn compact. The oath was taken in the Governor's house on the 12th of June, 1535, in the presence of many persons, the priest saying mass, and the two governors having put their right hands above the consecrated hands of the priest which held "the most holy sacrament."   This was called "dividing the Host;" and was considered a most solemn form of declaring friendship.

The Mariscal now resolved to enter his own

territory, where he could be free from the Pizarros; and accordingly he prepared to march into Chili, which certainly fell within the confines of his government. In making preparations for his departure he lavished his resources, giving those who would follow him money to buy arms and horses, upon the simple understanding that they would repay him from their gains in the country where they were going. As he was now greatly popular, his service was readily embraced, and some even of those who had *repartimientos* at Cusco resolved to throw them up and follow the Mariscal. The Inca placed at his disposal the services of his brother Paullo and of the high-priest Villaoma, who were ordered to accompany Almagro into Chili. These he sent on before; he himself was to go next; and his lieutenant-general Rodrigo Orgoñez was to follow with the rest of the people. It may show how much Almagro's service was sought after, that so distinguished a person in Pizarro's camp as Fernando de Soto was greatly disappointed at not having been named lieutenant-general of the Mariscal's forces.

Almagro, the day before his departure, is said

to have begged Pizarro to send his brothers back
to Castille, saying that for that end he would be
willing that Pizarro should give them from the
joint estate whatever amount of treasure he
pleased; that such a course would give general
content in the land, for " there was no one whom
those gentlemen would not insult, relying upon
their relationship to him."   To this request
Pizarro replied, that his brothers respected and
loved him as a father, and that they would give
no occasion of scandal.*

---

* Oviedo describes Fernando Pizarro in the following
words : " And of all those (the brothers Pizarro) Fernando
Pizarro was the only one of a legitimate bed, and the most
imbedded in pride.   He was a stout man of lofty stature,
with a large tongue and heavy lips, and the end of the nose
very fleshy and red ; and this man was the disturber of the
quiet of all, and especially of the two ancient associates
Francisco Pizarro and Diego de Almagro."

CHAPTER II.

Fernando Pizarro returns from Spain—Takes the Command at Cusco—Flight and Rebellion of the Inca Manco— Description of Cusco.

AS the brotherhood of the Pizarros is about to play a very important part in the history, it is desirable to consider what the advantages and disadvantages would have been of such a course as Almagro counselled. It is true that the promotion of near relatives is, and always has been, a very offensive thing to those who are hoping for advancement from any man in power, or even to those who are merely looking on at his proceedings. But, on the other hand, near relatives, though often more difficult to act with than other men, are nearly sure to be faithful. The certainty of this faithfulness has, doubtless, weighed much with men like Pizarro, newly and suddenly possessed of power; and it was a difficult question for him to decide, whether in his case it was not wise to endure the odium for the sake of the fidelity. Moreover, Pizarro's brothers were all of them good soldiers and brave men. Fernando was a most skilful captain; Gonzalo was said to be "the best lance" that had come to the Indies; Juan showed his valour at the siege of Cusco; and Martin afterwards died fighting by his brother's side.

The Marquis, unwilling to deprive himself of the services of such brothers, would not listen to the counsels of the Mariscal in this matter; which counsels, however, have been held by commentators to be very sagacious.

The Governor of Nueva Toledo (Almagro) set out to conquer the country that had been assigned to him: the Governor of Nueva Castilla, for that was the name of Pizarro's province, returned to superintend the building of his new town, Los Reyes. Juan Pizarro was left in command at Cusco. It was soon after the reconciliation of the two Governors that Fernando Pizarro returned from the Court of Spain. He had undertaken to raise a benevolence for the court from the colonists of Peru.

In order to obtain the sum required from Cusco, and also to keep the Indians quiet (for an uncle of Manco Inca had been lately rebelling and endeavouring to persuade his nephew to join in the rebellion), Pizarro resolved to send his brother Fernando to supersede Juan in the government of that city. It is said that the Marquis had respect also to any danger there might be from the smothered discontent of the Mariscal or his followers, and, therefore, wished to have a person of Fernando's weight and authority at the city, which was nearest to Almagro's province. Fernando did not hesitate to treat the Inca with much favour, although there appeared a good deal of dissatisfaction among the Indians in the neighbourhood. An Indian, named Villaoma (whom the Peruvians held in the same veneration in which the Spaniards held the pope), now returned to Cusco from having attended the Mariscal, with whom he had gone as captain of the Indian forces. News came of a revolt of the district of Collao; still the Inca was not suspected of being concerned in it; nay, leave was given him to go out of the

city of Cusco to receive Villaoma on his return.
Thereupon the two great Indian authorities, the
Inca and the High Priest, returned together into
Cusco, and both went straight to the Temple of
the Sun; and there, according to Valverde, Villaoma not only complained of the injuries he had
received when with Almagro, but counselled revolt.   Fernando Pizarro, however, had no sus-
picion of this plot, for two days afterwards he
gave permission to the Inca, and to many of
the chiefs, to go to a valley where his father
was buried, in order to perform the customary
annual rites at his tomb.

On the 18th of April, 1536, the Inca, with
Villaoma, went out of Cusco, leaving behind them
some of the principal chiefs, who were suspected
by the Spaniards.   This he did for a blind to his
real purpose.   He had been absent only two days,
when a Spaniard arrived in the city to inform
Fernando Pizarro that the Inca was going to
Ares, fifteen leagues distant, in a very mountainous district; from which circumstance it might,
he thought, be concluded he was about to revolt.
Fernando Pizarro merely sent a message to the
Inca, begging him to hasten his return, in order

to accompany him on an expedition to chastise the caciques of Collao, who were in rebellion (Atahuallpa was right in fearing to lose the presence of this Fernando); but the Inca took no heed of this message. On the contrary, being now within the protection of this rugged country, he was enabled to proclaim his designs in all their fulness. A great assembly was held of the caciques and other principal persons of the district; and it may be imagined what orations, full of grief, shame, and lamentation, were uttered on that occasion. Never had an assemblage of men greater reason to complain, greater injuries to redress. Their kings dethroned, their temples profaned, their priests expelled, their sacred virgins scorned and violated, their property seized, themselves, their lands, their wives, and their children given away, in a strange kind of captivity* amongst this victorious band of strangers, —what eloquence that rage or hate could give would be wanting? It is unlikely that any Peruvian chief who spoke on that day was one who had not received some deadly domestic in-

---

* The system of *Encomiendas.*

jury, something of the kind which Christians even can hardly pretend to forgive—and which the Spanish Christians of that day would certainly have thought it a sacred duty to revenge. That dusky assemblage might have been seen, waving to and fro with emotions of horror and hatred, as the chiefs stood upon some level arid spot, with the burning sun pouring down upon them, to whom each fiery speaker would appeal, as to a god, injured, desecrated, and maddened, like themselves.

There can be little doubt that the most ardent and earnest appeals were made on this occasion to the valour, the piety, and the revengefulness of the Peruvian Indians, for a solemn pledge was taken, which the assembly could only have been prepared for by such adjurations. The Inca commanded that two large golden vessels, full of wine, should be brought before him; and then he said, " I am determined not to leave a Christian alive in all this land; wherefore I intend, in the first place, to besiege Cusco. Whoever among you resolves to serve me in this design has to stake his life upon it. Let him drink." In this manner, and with no other condition, many captains and principal persons rose and drank; nor could it be said that they did not afterwards fulfil their part in all the dangers and toils which this fatal draught imposed upon them.

The city of Cusco was worthy of being the spot which elicited the last great effort of the Peruvians to rid themselves of their invaders. There is no capital in Europe that has been constructed on so grand a plan. Cusco was, as it were, a microcosm of the whole empire. As the men of different tribes came up from Antisuyo, Condesuyo, Collasuyo, and Chinchasuyo, they ranged themselves in the outskirts adjacent to the four quarters of the town corresponding with these four divisions of the empire; and each tribe took up its position as nearly as possible in the same geographical order which it held in its own country. The tribe that was to the north of it in its own country was to the north of it also in Cusco. Each tribe, also, had an especial head-dress, and was discernible from all the rest, either by a difference in the colour of the sash wound round the head, or by a difference in the colour of the feathers. The Inca, in traversing his city, was thus enabled to review every section of his empire, and to recognize the inhabitants of each district at a glance.

The greater part of the houses in the city were constructed, either wholly or partly, of stone, though some were built of bricks burnt in the sun.   Two streams entered Cusco, and traversed the city.   They entered under bridges, with flood-gates, to prevent inundation.   These streams, in their passage through the city, had beds of masonry to run in, so that the water might always be clear and clean.   One of the streams passed through the great square.   A huge fortress over-awed the city.   The stones, or rather rocks, of which the demi-lunes and other parts of the fortress were constructed, seemed of Cyclopean work.   The Spaniards said that not even "the bridge of Segovia, or the other buildings which Hercules and the Romans had made, were worthy to be compared to the citadel of Cusco."   An eye-witness says, "I measured a stone at Tia-guanaco, thirty-eight feet long, eighteen feet broad, and about six feet thick; but in the wall of the fortress of Cusco, which is constructed of masonry, there are many stones of much greater size."   It appears, from modern research, that some of these stones were fifty feet long, twenty-two feet broad, and six feet thick. How they were conveyed thither is a problem which has exercised ingenious men ever since the conquest. But the works of despotic monarchs of the olden time, who could employ an army to fetch a single stone, have always astonished more civilized nations, accustomed to a reasonable economy in the use of human labour.

It seems that cement was used by the Peruvians; but the work at Cusco was so exquisitely finished that none of this cement was visible, for the masonry appeared " as smooth as a table." This, however, was only at the junction of the stones; the rest of the stonework was left in the same state as it had been when taken from the quarry. Part of the fortress was an immense arsenal, which, under the rule of the Incas, had contained large stores of arms and accoutrements of all kinds—also of metals, such as tin, lead, silver and gold.

On a hill which overlooked the city, there were certain small towers that served as gnomons, and were used for solar observations.

In Cusco and its environs, including the whole

valley which could be seen from the top of the tower, it is said that there were a hundred thousand houses. Amongst these were shops and storehouses, and places for the reception of tribute. A strange practice of the Peruvians may account in some measure for this enormous extent of building. It appears that when the great lords died, their houses were not occupied by their successors, but were, nevertheless, not suffered to fall into decay; and an establishment was kept up in them, in honour of the deceased master.

There was a large vacant space left in the town for the erection of future palaces, it being the custom for every reigning Inca to build a new palace.

The great Temple of the Sun had, before the Spaniards rifled Cusco, been a building of singular gorgeousness. The interior was plated with gold; and on each side of the central image of the Sun were ranged the embalmed bodies of the Incas, sitting upon their golden thrones raised upon pedestals of gold. All round the outside of the building, at the top of the walls ran a coronal of gold about three feet in depth. Adjacent to the Temple of the Sun were other buildings, also beautifully adorned, which had been dedicated to the moon, the stars, to thunder, lightning, and the rainbow. Each of these minor buildings had its appropriate paintings and adornments. Then there were the schools of the learned Amautas and the Haravecs, or poets, which might be entered by a private way from the palace of the Inca Roca, who had delighted to listen to the discourses of the wise men of his dominions.

Cusco, independently of its temples and its palaces and its court, was in itself an object of fond admiration to the Peruvians; and, as Garcilaso declares, it was to them what Rome was to the rest of the world.*

Such was the city, not less dear because dishonoured and disfigured, that Manco Inca and his brave companions in arms had pledged themselves to regain.

---

* Pedro de Cieça, one of the persons who saw Cusco within the first twenty years after the Spanish conquest, says " Cusco was grand and stately: it must have been founded by a people of great intelligence."—PEDRO DE CIEÇA, *Chronica del Peru*, parte i. cap. 92.

CHAPTER III.

The Siege of Cusco by the Revolted Peruvians.

FERNANDO PIZARRO, having been soon informed that Manco Inca really had revolted, far from awaiting the attack, lost no time in making an endeavour to seize upon the Inca's person. The friendly heights, however, protected the Indian sovereign, and Pizarro could not come near him. There were now many skirmishes near Ares between the Spaniards and the Peruvians, in which the slaughter of the Inca's forces was immense. Still the Indians, from all their four provinces, Chinchasuyo, Collasuyo, Condesuyo, and Antisuyo, came pouring in upon the scene of action. On the heights the Indians began to prevail, though in the plains, where the Spanish cavalry could act, it was like a company of butchers amid innumerable flocks of sheep. In one of these skirmishes the Indians, who were beginning to learn the craft of war, retreated until they led their enemies into an ambuscade, where no less than twenty thousand Indians poured down upon the Spaniards. The ground was so rough that the horses were disabled from acting, and though Juan and Gonzalo Pizarro did all that they could to retrieve the day, they were obliged to withdraw their forces into the city. Their Indian followers, who had been stationed in the fortress commanding Cusco, were driven out of it; and it was occupied by the enemy. But Fernando Pizarro, one of the most valiant men, not only of the captains in America, but of any in that age, beat back the pursuers and regained the fortress. Juan Pizarro was wounded in this battle.

The whole aspect of affairs now began to look very threatening for the Spaniards. A question arose whether it would be better to occupy the fortress or to abandon it to the enemy. Juan Pizarro contended that it should be abandoned, arguing that if the Indians were to occupy the fortress, the Spaniards could retake it whenever they pleased, and that it would be unwise to divide their small force. This advice seemed to be judicious, and was adopted.

Fernando Pizarro now resolved to form his horsemen into three " companies," placing each company under a captain. He had but ninety horsemen, and he gave thirty to each of the three commanders, committing to his guard a third part of the town. To the foot-soldiers he did not assign any especial part of the town to defend, because they were very few, and the enemy made little account of them. The next day, being Saturday, the Feast of " St. John before the Latin Gate," when the garrison awoke, they found the fortress occupied by the hostile Indians; and then the siege of Cusco may be said to have commenced. The disproportion of numbers was immense. There may have been one or two thousand Indian auxiliaries attached to the Spanish cause; but the besiegers, as was afterwards ascertained, amounted to a hundred thousand warriors and eighty thousand attendants for camp-service. They immediately set fire to those houses, which lay between the fortress and the town; and, under cover of this fire, they continued to gain ground, making barricades in the streets, and digging holes, so that the cavalry could not act against them.

It is impossible not to sympathise in some measure with the Peruvians, and to rejoice whenever they obtain any success on their side, so that, if only for a moment, the tide of war is turned against those remorseless missionaries, the Spaniards. On this day, which was probably the last on which the natives in all that vast continent had any real chance of disembarrassing themselves of their invaders, not only fire, but air, came to the aid of the weaker side. There was, fortunately for them, a high wind, and the roofs being of straw or rushes, the fire spread so rapidly that at one moment it appeared as if the whole city were one sheet of flame. The war-cries of the assailants were appalling. The smoke was so dense that sight and hearing were alike confused. But the Spaniards were not men to be easily daunted. Each captain held his ground in his own quarter, where, however, the Indians pressed in upon them in such a manner that they could do no more than hold their ground, having scarcely room to fight.   Fernando Pizarro was to be seen, now in one quarter, now in another, wherever the distress was greatest.   The Indians, who supposed that the day was really theirs, threw themselves with the greatest bravery into the streets, fighting hand to hand with the Spaniards; displaying that desperate valour which takes no heed of the inequality of weapons, and giving blows which they must have been aware would be returned on the instant with a hundredfold the vigour and effect that there could be in their own.

Fernando Pizarro saw that, without some change in the mode of resistance, all was lost for the Spaniards.   Drawing, therefore, from each company, a few men, amounting altogether to only twenty, he made a sally on the road to Condesuyo; and, coming round upon the Indians from that quarter, charged them vigorously and drove them back with great slaughter to the rough part of the sierra, where they again reformed their ranks and renewed the battle. Still, however, the ardour of the fight did not abate in the central part of the city, to which Fernando Pizarro returned to resume his command-in-chief.

There was still no rest for the Spaniards. The city continued to burn. The Indian High Priest, Villaoma, who was likewise the General, occupied and maintained the fortress. In the city, as the houses were burnt, the Indians mounted upon the blackened walls, and moving along them were enabled, in that favourable position, to press on the attack. Thence they could deride all the efforts of horsemen to dislodge them. So the contest continued for days. Neither by day nor by night did they give any rest to the Spaniards, who were obliged to make perpetual sallies in order to throw down walls, destroy barricades, fill up great holes, and break up channels by which the Indians were letting water in upon them, so as to produce an artificial inundation. Thus for six days the warfare continued, until the Indians gained nearly the whole of the city, the Spaniards being able only to hold the great square, and some houses which surrounded it.

Many of the Spaniards now began to look upon their cause as hopeless. Flight by means of their horses was comparatively easy; and there were not wanting those who counselled the abandonment of the city, and the attempt to save their own lives, if it could be accomplished by this sacrifice. Fernando Pizarro, who was as great in counsel as in war, with a smile replied, "I do not know, señores, why you wish to do this, for in my mind there is not, and there has not been, any fear." From shame they did not dare to declare their thoughts in his presence, and so the matter passed off until the evening, when he summoned the chief Spaniards together, and, with a serene countenance, he thus addressed them: "I have called you together, señores, because it appears to me that the Indians each day disgrace us more and more, and I believe that the cause of this is the weakness that there is in some of us, which is no little, since you openly maintain that we should give up the city. Wherefore, if you, Juan Pizarro, give such an opinion, how is it that you had courage to defend the city against Almagro, when he sought to rebel? and as for you," turning to the treasurer, "it would appear a very ugly thing for you to talk in this fashion, since you have charge of the royal fifths, and are obliged to give account of them with the same obligation that he is to give account of the fortress. For you other señores, who are alcaldes and regidors, to whom the execution of the laws is committed in this city, it is not for you to commit such a great folly that you should deliver it into the hands of these tyrants."

Words have been often misused in speeches, but never more, perhaps, than in calling the Peruvians, who came to take possession of their own, " these tyrants."

Then he spoke of his own duties. " It would be a sad tale to tell of me," he exclaimed, " were it to be said that Fernando Pizarro, from any motive of fear, had abandoned the territory which his brother, Don Francisco Pizarro, had conquered and colonized. Wherefore, gentlemen, in the service of God and of the King, sustaining your houses and your estates, die, rather than desert them. If I am left alone, I will pay with my life the obligation which lies upon me, rather than have it said that another gained the city, and that I lost it." He then reminded them of the commonplace remark, " that with vigour that which appears impossible is gained, and without vigour even that which is easy appears difficult."

The courage of the assembled Spaniards answered to this bold appeal; and, as it was now agreed upon to defend the city to the utmost, Fernando did not hesitate in putting the worst before them. He said, " The men are worn out, the horses are exhausted, and, in the state in which we are, it is impossible to hold the city two days longer, wherefore it is necessary to lose all our lives or to gain the fortress. That being gained, the city is secure. To-morrow morning I must go with all the horsemen that can be mustered, and take that fortress." They answered that the horsemen were ready to a man, to die with him, or to succeed in that enterprise. Upon this, Juan Pizarro, wounded as he was, claimed the principal part in the next day's action, saying, " It was my fault that the fortress was not occupied, and I said that I would take it whenever it should be necessary to do so. Ill would it, therefore, appear, if while I am alive any other person should undertake the duty for me."

Fernando Pizarro consented. This question of leadership being settled, and two subordinates having been chosen, Juan Pizarro lost no time in selecting a company of fifty men for the work of the morrow, the three captains being himself, his brother Gonzalo, and a cavalier named Fernando Ponce.

Very early in the morning the fifty men, with their leaders, were drawn up in the great square. Fernando Pizarro addressed some parting advice to his brother Juan,—namely, that, when out of the town, he should take the royal road from Cusco to Los Reyes, and should not turn until he had gone about a league, for, although the fortress was very near, so many holes had been dug, and barricades thrown up by the Indians, that there was no hope of taking the fortress except by coming round on the far side of it.

Fernando Pizarro had hardly finished giving this advice, when a body of Indians came down with the intent of taking a fort which had been made as a place of refuge from the great square, and which overlooked the whole of it. The two sentinels on guard at this fort were asleep — a thing not to be wondered at, considering the fatigues of the last few days,—and before any succour could be given, the Indians had mastered the fort. The day, therefore, began with an ill omen for the Spaniards.

Fernando Pizarro ordered in great haste some

active foot-soldiers to retake this fort, which they soon succeeded in doing. When this had been accomplished, Fernando united all his forces, horse and foot, to gain possession of a very strong barricade which the Indians had thrown up, in order to prevent the Spaniards from going out of the city in the direction of the plain. A body of twenty thousand Indians from the district of Chinchasuyo kept this barricade. It was fortunate for the Spaniards that the Indians had not delayed their attack upon the fort until a little later in the day, for, by this movement towards the barricade, Fernando Pizarro was obliged to leave the great square nearly undefended. But the main body of the Indians had not yet come down from their quarters to commence their usual attacks upon the city.

When the Chinchasuyans who had the charge of the barricade saw the Spaniards advancing upon them in full force, some of them shouted out to one another, " Those Christians who have the good horses are flying, and the others which remain are the sick. Let us allow these to draw off, and then we shall be able to kill them all." This plan of suffering the Spaniards to divide

their forces may have had some effect in weaken-
ing the resistance of the Indians at the barricade;
still they fought on with great bravery, but they
could not prevent the fifty horsemen making their
way out of the city. The rest of the Spaniards
returned with all haste to the grand square; for
a column of the enemy—from the same division,
I conjecture, which had once captured the fort in
the morning—came down again to make another
attack on it, having seen or heard the skirmish
at the Chinchasuyan barricade. Fernando Pizarro, whose part in the conflict it was to make
decisive charges on critical occasions, rushed out
with his men, and soon put the Indians to flight,
for, as the main body of the enemy was still asleep
in their quarters, this one watchful division could
not alone resist Pizarro's charge.

Meanwhile Juan Pizarro had conducted his
men along the royal road to Los Reyes; and,
after proceeding as far as had been previously
agreed upon, had turned to the right, had fought
his way along the ridges wherever he had encountered any enemy, had come down upon the
open ground before the fortress, and so established
a communication between himself and his brother

in the city.   The Indians posted between the fortress and the city decamped, some throwing themselves into the fortress, and others into other strong positions.

The communication was now so complete, that Fernando Pizarro was able to reinforce his brother with all the Spanish foot-soldiers and the friendly Indians.   At the same time he sent Juan word on no account to make the attack upon the fortress until nightfall, for the enemy were so many, and the position so strong, that the Spaniards could gain no honour in the attack. Fernando also begged his brother not to adventure his own person in the fight; for on account of the wound which Juan had already received, he could not put on his morion, and Fernando said it would be absolute madness to go into battle without that.   Juan Pizarro did not adopt his brother's advice; for though he made a show of preparation as if he were going to bivouac upon the plain for the night, it was only a feint, and when he saw that the Indians were less on their guard, he gave orders for a sudden attack upon some strong positions in front of the fortress.   Gonzalo Pizarro was entrusted with a troop to make this attack. When the Indians saw the Spaniards moving upwards, they came down upon them in such a multitude, that Gonzalo Pizarro and his men could not even succeed in approaching these fortified outposts. Indeed, the Spaniards began to give way before the weight of numbers, when Juan Pizarro, " not being able to endure" this check, hurried onwards to support his brother. The men, animated by this sight, for Juan and Gonzalo fought in the front rank, rushed forwards, and succeeded in taking these strong positions, so that they found themselves now under the walls of the principal building. Juan Pizarro, not satisfied with this partial success, made a bold dash at the entrance into the fortress. This entrance was an outwork projecting from the body of the fortress, enclosed on each side by two low walls, but open at the top, so that it might be thoroughly commanded from the battlements, having an outer gate corresponding with the principal gate of the fortress. The walls which formed this outwork had roofs to them, doubtless in order that those of the besieged who had to defend the post might be under cover, while their assailants were exposed to missiles from the higher parts of the building. Beneath this outwork the crafty Indians had recently dug a deep pitfall. But, unfortunately for them, as they came flying in from the pursuit of the Spaniards, they fell one upon another, heaped together in such a manner that " they filled up with their own bodies that which their own hands had made." Juan Pizarro, still fighting in front, advanced upon this road made for him by the bodies of his enemies; but just as he entered, a stone, hurled from the heights of the fortress, descended upon his unprotected head, and laid him senseless on the spot. His men recovered, and bore off the body of their commander, in which life was not extinct; though the wound was of a fatal nature, for Juan Pizarro never rose from his couch again.

After this great check, Gonzalo Pizarro, on whom the command had now devolved, did what he could to reanimate his men; but his efforts were of no avail. The numbers of the enemy brought to bear upon the points of attack continued to increase, and the Spaniards were obliged to draw off from the fortress. The following morning, however, the indomitable Fernando made a circuit of the stronghold of the Indians, and, seeing that it was surrounded by a very high wall, came to the conclusion, that, without scaling-ladders, there was no hope of taking the place. The whole of the day, therefore, was spent in making scaling-ladders by all those who could be spared for that service. They were not many who could be spared, for the enemy gave Gonzalo Pizarro and Fernando Ponce no rest all day, endeavouring to force the strong position which these commanders occupied. The Indians in the fortress did all they could by words and signs to animate their friends, even calling by name upon particular chiefs to come to the rescue; but the Spaniards maintained their positions.

That day Fernando Pizarro was to be seen everywhere throughout the Spanish quarters. He knew that not only the existence of all the Spaniards who were there, but that the security of the Spanish empire in that part of the world was in peril. Here, he hurried with his small party of reserve, and left them; there, alone, he threw himself into some post where the effect of his personal presence was wanted. The contest grew so furious and the shouts so loud (the Indians, like all partially civilized people, were great shouters in war), that it seemed " as if the whole world was there in fiercest conflict."

The Inca, whose position was at a spot about three leagues distance from Cusco, was not inactive. Knowing that the fortress was besieged, and being as well aware as Pizarro how important the possession of that stronghold was, he sent a reinforcement of five thousand of his best soldiers. These fresh troops pressed the Spaniards very hard. They not only fought with the animation of untired men; but all the energy that fanaticism could give them, was called forth to succour Villaoma, their Chief Priest, who was within the fortress.

In the city itself the battle languished, for though some encounters took place there in the course of the day, the best part of the Indian troops were fighting round the fortress. This was an oversight on the part of the Indian generals. More pressure on the Spanish posts in the grand square would have compelled the withdrawal of some of the Spaniards engaged in investing the fortress; and when the contending parties are greatly unequal in point of numbers, to multiply the points of attack is a mode of warfare which must tell disastrously against the less numerous party.

The day went on without either side having apparently gained or lost much. But the Spaniards had maintained their positions, while the scaling-ladders were being made. These being finished, Fernando Pizarro and the foot-soldiers commenced their attack at the hour of vespers. This was an excellent disposition of the troops. The horsemen could fight, as they had been fighting all day, to clear the ground about the place, while the hardy foot-soldiers, fitter for the work of scaling the fortress, must have seemed almost a new enemy to the beleaguered Indians. Fernando and his men pressed up to the walls with the utmost fury and determination. The conflict had now lasted about thirty hours, and the reinforcements of Indians had not succeeded in making their way into the fortress. The succour most wanted there was fresh ammunition. Stones and darts began to grow scarce amongst the besieged; and Villaoma, seeing the fury of his new enemies, resolved to fly. Communicating his intentions to some of his friends, with them he made his way out of the fortress at the part which looked towards the river. The ground there was very precipitous, but there were some winding passages in the rocks, so constructed that they were invisible to the Spaniards below, but which were known to the Peruvians. Taking this secret route, Villaoma and his friends made good their flight, without being perceived by the Spaniards; and, when beyond the walls of the fortress, Villaoma collected and drew off the division of his army which consisted of the Chinchasuyan Indians. From thence the recreant High Priest went to his master the Inca, who, when he heard the ill news, was ready to die of grief.

At the time Villaoma fled, the fortress was not altogether lost. In it there remained an Indian chief of great estimation amongst his people, one of those who had drunk out of the golden vases, and with whom were all the rest of the gallant men who had pledged themselves in the like simple but solemn manner. The whole night through these devoted men maintained their position. Fernando Pizarro's efforts throughout those eventful hours were such as desperation only could inspire; and, as the day dawned, he had the satisfaction of perceiving that the defence of the Indians began to slacken, not that their brave hearts were daunted, but that the magazine of stones and arrows was fairly exhausted.

The fate of the beleaguered Indians was now clear to all beholders, to none clearer than to themselves; still this nameless captain gave no signs of surrender. " There is not written of any Roman such a deed as he did." These are the honest words of the Spanish narrator. Traversing all parts of the fortress with a club in his hand, wherever he saw one of his warriors who was giving way, he struck him down, and hurled his body upon the besiegers. He himself had two arrows in him, of which he took no more account than if they were not there. Seeing at last that it was not an Indian here and there who was giving way, but that the whole of his men were exhausted, and that the Spaniards were pressing up on the scaling-ladders at all points, he perceived that the combat was hopeless. One weapon alone remained to him, his club. That he dashed down upon the besiegers; and then, as a last expression of despair, taking earth in his hands, he bit it, and rubbed his face with it,* " with such signs of anguish and heartsickness as cannot be described." Having thus expressed his rage and his despair, resolving not to behold the enemy's entrance, he hurled himself, the last thing he had to hurl, from the height down upon the invaders, that they might not triumph over him, and that he might fulfil the pledge he had given when he drank from the golden vases. The hero of the Indians having thus perished, no pretence of further resistance could be made. Fernando Pizarro and his men made good their entrance, and disgraced their victory by putting the besieged to the sword, who were in number above fifteen hundred.

Such was the dismay occasioned among the Peruvians by the capture of the fortress, that they deserted their positions near the city, and retired to their encampments, which were well fortified. The next morning Fernando Pizarro

---

* " And they rent every one his mantle, and sprinkled pust upon their heads toward heaven."—*Job* ii. 12.

sallied forth and became the assailant, and the slaughter of the Peruvians was immense, day after day.

It was, however, soon found that the Indians had desisted from attacking the city not from ill-success only, but from being called away by certain religious ceremonies; for, having completed their sacrificial rites, they recommenced the siege, but this time under very different auspices. The Spaniards now not only occupied the fortress, but had extended their works beyond the city; and the Indians were not able to gain an entrance into any part of it. This second and futile siege lasted twenty days, when the new moon again compelled them to withdraw to perform their religious rites. Fernando Pizarro again became the assailant, and the slaughter of the Peruvians was immense; yet, upon the completion of their ceremonial sacrifices, they again returned; when the Spanish commander took a terrible resolve. He gave orders to all his men that they should slay every Indian woman they came up with, in order that the survivors might not dare to come and serve their husbands and their children. This cruel scheme was so successful, that the Indians abandoned the siege, fearing to lose their wives, and the wives fearing death.

Fernando Pizarro was now at liberty to ascertain what had become of his brother the Marquis at Los Reyes. He had already conceived it probable that Los Reyes had been invested at the same time as Cusco. It was possible that his brother had not been able to drive back the besiegers. The Spaniards, in their attacks upon the Indians who were now retreating, came upon some fragments of letters that had been seized by them, and found that succour had been sent from Los Reyes; and, by torture, they learned further that various parties had been sent to their aid during the siege, which had all been intercepted; and that the Inca had, as trophies, two hundred heads of Christians, and one hundred and fifty skins of horses. The Indians who were tortured believed, likewise, that the Governor with all his people had embarked from Los Reyes and deserted the country.

But Francisco Pizarro was not reduced to such straits as those.

When, indeed, at the beginning of the siege of Cusco, the various parties, amounting to two hundred men and a great number of horses, which he had sent to the assistance of his brothers, were cut off, and he could gain no intelligence whatever from Cusco, he felt his position to be most critical. He summoned back one of his principal captains, whom he had sent in another direction. He wrote to Panamá, Nicaragua, Guatemala, New Spain, and to the *audiencia* in Hispaniola, praying for instant succour. Indeed, he offered Alvarado that, if he would come to his rescue, he would leave him the land of Peru, and would himself return to Panamá or Spain.

Meanwhile the Indians, to the number of fifty thousand, and under the command of a great chief named Teyyupangui, began to invest Los Reyes. Pizarro made his preparations. The Indians advanced towards the town, and forced their way over the walls and into the streets; their general, with a lance in his hand, advancing in front of his men. But, as the ground was level, the Spanish cavaliers were enabled to act with all the tremendous superiority which their arms, their horses, and their armour gave them. Their success was instantaneous. Unfortunately for the Indians, Teyyupangui and the principal men who surrounded him were slain in this first encounter. The loss of their general entirely dispirited the Indian forces. The Spaniards, following up their advantage, drove the enemy back to the foot of the sierra which overlooked the town; and Pizarro, on the succeeding night, would have stormed the heights where the Indians had taken refuge; but he received intelligence that they had broken up their camp, and had fled. This was the end of the siege of Los Reyes.

Immediate steps were now taken for the relief of Fernando Pizarro at Cusco; but, as the number of men that could be spared was but small, the commander was not to move on to Cusco until he should receive reinforcements.

In the meantime, Fernando Pizarro had delivered himself, and supposing himself to be alone in the country, had not ceased to press the Indians with all the vigour possible. The result was that the Indians began to give up the contest.

Rumours now arose that Almagro was returning from Chili. This was first communicated by the Indian captives, and they threatened Fernando Pizarro and his men, saying that the Adelantado was coming, and he was their friend, and intended to kill all the Spaniards of Cusco. And in about two months' time there arrived certain intelligence that the Adelantado, with five hundred Spaniards, was within seven leagues of Cusco.

The conquest of Peru may be said to have been now completed. The sieges of Cusco and Los Reyes show that it was not such an easy task as some historians have supposed; they manifest great valour on the part of the Peruvian Indians, and, moreover, give an instance, of the many to be met with, that the second great resistance of a conquered people is often the most difficult to overcome. The internal dissensions of the Peruvians, which were at their height when Pizarro first arrived in the country, must be considered as having furnished no slight aid to the Spaniards; and. in the absence of such dissensions, the conquest might have been deferred for many years. Each year the Peruvians would have attained more skill in resisting horsemen; and, as it has been observed before, horses were the chief means of conquest which the Spaniards possessed. How completely the Peruvians were dismayed by horses may be inferred from the fact that, when they had these animals in their power, they put them to death, instead of attempting to make use of them. There is no good evidence to show that a single horse was spared, when the Inca's troops succeeded in overpowering the cavalry that was sent by Pizarro to reinforce his brothers at Cusco.

CHAPTER IV.

Almagro returns from Chili, claims Cusco—Fernando Pizarro negotiates with him—Almagro treacherously enters Cusco by night—Imprisons the brothers Pizarro, and defeats Francisco Pizarro's commander, Alonzo de Alvarado.

THE return of Almagro from Chili was not much to be wondered at. From the first landing of Pizarro, to the taking of Cusco, the advance of the Spaniards had been little other than a triumphant march. Conquerors had been borne along in hammocks on the shoulders of obsequious Indians, to rifle temples plated with gold: but the advance into Chili was an enterprise of a different kind. Almagro and his men went by the sierras and returned by the plains. In both journeys they had great hardships to suffer. In the snowy passes men and horses had been frozen to death; and on their return by the plain they had been obliged to traverse a horrible region, called the desert of Atacáma, which could only be passed with the greatest difficulty.

On what pretext did they return, as there were no new circumstances to justify such a course? The despatches from Spain, appointing Almagro governor of New Toledo, only reached him after he had commenced his journey into Chili; but he had been informed of their contents before, and he had taken that solemn oath, when the host was broken by the two governors, in perfect cognizance of his rights. The revolt of the Indians was made known to him; but it cannot be for a moment assumed that this was the real cause of his return.

It is very likely that the question of the limits of his government was often renewed and discussed by his men and officers in the course of their march and over their watch-fires, and being discussed with all the passion and prejudice of eager partisans, it is very probable that there was not a man in Almagro's little army who did not think that Cusco fell within the limits of his commander's government. Their misery doubt-less sharpened their prejudices, and Almagro's weary, frost-bitten men must have sighed for the palatial splendours and luxuries of Cusco; which they had foolishly given up, as they would have said, to these Pizarros. Even the mines of Po-tosi, had they been aware of their existence, would hardly have proved a sufficient inducement to detain Almagro's men in Chili. But Potosi was as yet undiscovered, and Cusco was well known to every individual in the army. Under such circumstances, the Mariscal's return may be set down as faithless, treacherous, or unwise, but it cannot be considered other than as most natural. A greater man than Almagro might have carried his companions onwards, but Almagro was chiefly great in bestowing largesses, and Chili afforded no scope for such a commander.

It must not be supposed that the question of the limits to Pizarro's government was an easy one, and that it was merely passion and prejudice, which decided, in the minds of Almagro's follow-ers, that Cusco fell within the province of New Toledo. There were several ways of reckoning the two hundred and seventy-five leagues which had been assigned to Pizarro. They might be measured along the royal road. This would not have suited Pizarro's followers, who contended that the leagues were to be reckoned as the crow flies. " Even if so," replied Almagro's partisans, "the line is not to be drawn from north to south, but from east to west." They also contended that these leagues might be measured on the sea-coast, in which case the sinuosities of the coast line would have to be taken into account. In short, it was a question quite sufficiently dubious in itself to admit of prejudice coming in on both sides with all the appearance of judicial impartiality.

However that may be, Almagro and his men took the fatal step of returning to maintain their supposed rights, which step a nicer sense of honour would have told them that they had, whether wisely or not, abandoned, when they quitted Cusco.

The two counsellors who had most influence over Almagro's mind were men whose dispositions presented a strange and violent contrast. One was Diego de Alvarado, a person of the utmost nobility of nature and, at the same time, delicacy of character. The other adviser was Rodrigo de Orgoñez, a hard, fierce, fanatic soldier, who had served in the wars of Italy. The conduct of the governor varied according to the advice listened to from one or other of these widely-different counsellors. The mild counsels of Alvarado were listened to in the morning; and some unscrupulous deed, prompted probably by Orgoñez, was transacted in the evening.

What effect their approach must have had upon Fernando Pizarro and his immediate adherents may be easily imagined. For many months he and his men had scarcely known what it was to have two days of rest. The efforts of the Indians were now slackening; and just at this moment there arrived an enemy who was to replace the softly-clad and poorly-armed Indians by men with arms, spirit, and accoutrements equal to those of the Spaniards of Cusco, and in numbers greatly superior.

The first movement, however, of the Mariscal was not directed against the Spaniards in Cusco. Previously to attacking them he strove to come to terms with their enemy, the Inca Manco. Had he succeeded in this politic design, he would then have been able to combine the Inca's forces with his own, and would also have had the appearance of having intervened to settle the war between the Indians and the Spaniards. This plan, however, failed. Meanwhile Fernando Pizarro had made several attempts to negotiate with Almagro, or at least to penetrate his designs. He endeavoured, by messengers, to lay before the Mariscal some of the motives which should regulate his conduct at this crisis, saying how much it would be for the service of God that peace should be maintained between them: if it were not, they would all be lost, and the Inca would remain lord of the whole country. He offered Almagro to receive him in the city with all honour, saying that Almagro's own quarters were prepared for him; but, before all things, Fernando Pizarro urged that a messenger might be sent to the Marquis, in order that he might come and settle matters amicably, and that, meanwhile, the Mariscal should enter the town with all his attendants. To this message an evasive reply was sent by Almagro, who, on a Monday, the 18th of April, 1537, made his appearance, with all his people, and pitched his camp at a league's distance from Cusco.

Fernando Pizarro invited him again to enter the city as a friend. To this Almagro haughtily replied, " Tell Fernando Pizarro that I am not going to enter the city, except as mine, or to lodge in any lodgings but those where he is,"— meaning that he would occupy the governor's apartments. Fernando Pizarro sent another message, pointing out to Almagro the danger to be apprehended from the revolted Indians, and begging that there might be amity between them until the Marquis should arrive. To this Almagro replied that he had authority from the king as governor, and that he was determined to enter Cusco. Having said this, Almagro advanced nearer, encamping within a crossbow shot of the city. Both sides now prepared for battle; but Fernando Pizarro, whose prudence throughout these transactions is very remarkable, called a council; and it was agreed by them that an alcalde with two regidors should go to Almagro's camp to demand of him, on the part of the Emperor, that he should not disturb the city, but that, if he had powers from his Majesty, he should present them before the council, in order that they might see whether his Majesty had conferred upon him the governorship of that city. As Fernando Pizarro had procured the powers, and brought them from Spain, he knew very well what they contained; but it was a reasonable request that the grounds upon which Almagro sought to enter the town should be laid before the governing body.

Almagro, especially if he listened at all to Diego de Alvarado, could not well refuse his assent to this proposition. Accordingly a truce was made for that day and until the next at noon. Early on the ensuing morning Almagro sent his powers to be laid before the Town Council, but demanded that Fernando Pizarro, as an interested party, should absent himself from the council. Fernando Pizarro conceded this point. The powers were formally laid before the alcaldes and the regidors, who, taking into council a graduate, perhaps Valverde himself, pronounced against Almagro's claims,—they desired that the division-line of the respective governments should be made, and that, until this should be settled by " pilots," Almagro should not give room for such a great scandal as forcing an entrance into the city, which they declared would be the ruin of all parties. " If," they said, " when the division has been settled, this city should fall within the limits of Almagro's government, they would be ready to receive him as governor, but upon any other footing they would not receive him."

Almagro, having received this spirited and sensible decision of the council, gave orders to his men, it being now mid-day, to prepare themselves for making an attack upon Cusco. Fernando Pizarro gave similar orders for the defence of the city. At this last moment the royal treasurer, and a licentiate named Prado, went out of the town and succeeded in prevailing upon Almagro to extend the time of the truce to the hour of vespers on the Wednesday in that same week, Almagro saying that he wished to prove how Cusco fell within his limits.

That evening Almagro, to his great dishonour, must have listened to his less scrupulous counsellor, for he resolved to surprise the city.

Fernando Pizarro, who was a perfect cavalier, was completely at his ease that night, expecting now that he and Almagro would be able to come to terms, until he should have time to let the Marquis know what was passing. At midnight there was a disturbance in Almagro's camp, it being given out that the bridges which led to the city were broken down. Immediately the soldiers shouted, " Almagro, Almagro! Let the traitors die!" and they rushed over all the four bridges, not one of which was broken down, into the great square. Thence they spread themselves into the streets, Orgoñez with a large body of troops making his way to the governor's apartments, still shouting, "Almagro, Almagro!" Fernando Pizarro was in bed when the alarm was given. He had time, however, to put on his armour. Fifteen men alone remained with him and his brother Gonzalo. Fernando placed himself at one door of the palace, Gonzalo at another; but the palace was as large as a church, and the doorways were proportionately large, without doors to them. The building was set on fire. Of their fifteen comrades several were cut down, fighting by their side, and it was not until the roof began to fall in that these brave Pizarros, overpowered by numbers, were overcome and made prisoners.

Almagro took formal possession of Cusco as its governor, and began to persecute those who held with the Pizarros. Meanwhile Alonzo de Alvarado, the commander whom Francisco Pizarro had sent out for the relief of Cusco from the Indians, was waiting at Xauxa for orders and reinforcements. Francisco Pizarro had now received men and arms from all parts of Spanish America. He lost no time in sending on these succours to Alonzo de Alvarado, and would have gone himself, but that the citizens of Los Reyes had insisted that, on account of his age, he should not undertake this expedition.

Alonzo de Alvarado, on his way to Cusco, learned what had happened there and how the Mariscal was now in possession of the city. Almagro, on his side, learned from Alvarado's letters to Fernando Pizarro that he was coming; and, not supposing that Alvarado knew of what had happened, sent a forged letter in Fernando Pizarro's name, to say that he had been able to maintain his position, and to suggest that Alvarado should take a certain route which he mentioned. This route Almagro knew would lead into a defile, where he hoped to be able to disarm Alvarado's men easily. Alvarado was only amused at such an attempt to deceive him. Al-

magro now tried by an embassage to treat with
Alonzo de Alvarado. Alvarado, though he wished
to show much courtesy to these friends of Almagro, and begged them to excuse him, took
away their arms, and placed them in confinement.

Almagro, receiving no answer to his embassage,
moved out from Cusco to the bridge of Abançay,
where Alonzo de Alvarado had taken up his
position. He had not omitted, since his occupation of Cusco, to attempt to come to terms
with the Peruvians. Failing, however, in nego-
tiating with Manco Inca he had given the *borla*
to Manco's brother Paullo, whose Indians now
proved very serviceable. At this juncture Alvarado sent fourteen horsemen to inform the Marquis
of all that had happened. There were many
desertions from Alvarado to Almagro's camp.
Pedro de Lerma, the second in command, went
over to Almagro, whose forces, independently of
the Indians, far outnumbered those of Alvarado.
After much fruitless negotiation nothing was left
but an appeal to arms. Accordingly, an attack
on Alvarado's position was made at nightfall.
The treachery of the men on that side was

flagrant, and Almagro had not much difficulty in gaining a complete victory. Alvarado surrendered, and narrowly escaped being put to death by Orgoñez.

Almagro's troops, flushed with success, declared that they would not leave one "*Pizarro*" (a slate) to stumble over. The counsel, given by Orgoñez, always the most uncompromising that could be thought of, was to kill the Pizarros and march at once to Los Reyes. The plan of marching upon Los Reyes was so far adopted, that it was proclaimed by sound of trumpet that all should prepare themselves for the march. There were, however, persons in Almagro's camp who had wives and families at Los Reyes, and they did not approve of this proposal. After the matter had remained two days in doubt it was resolved to return to Cusco. When they arrived there, Almagro issued a proclamation that no inhabitants of that city should make use of his Indians: for he, the Governor, suspended the *repartimientos*, as the Bishop of Cusco remarks, not wishing that any one should have anything for certain, until he himself should make the general *repartimiento*. This led to the greatest disorder, as no one had any certain interest in the welfare of any of the Indians, and consequently the Spaniards behaved to them with careless insolence and cruelty.* The next thing that was resolved upon at Cusco was for Orgoñez to make an attack upon the rebel Inca, which he did with great success, coming so close upon him that he made himself master of a golden ornament, called " the sun," which was greatly venerated among the Indians, and which Orgoñez brought home for Paullo. Thus, in every way Almagro's faction was triumphant.

------

* *Á rienda suelta*, " with loose bridle," as the Bishop says.

CHAPTER V.

Negotiations between the Marquis and the Mariscal respecting the Boundaries of their Governments — The Renewal of Hostilities—Fernando Pizarro takes the Command of his Brother's Army.

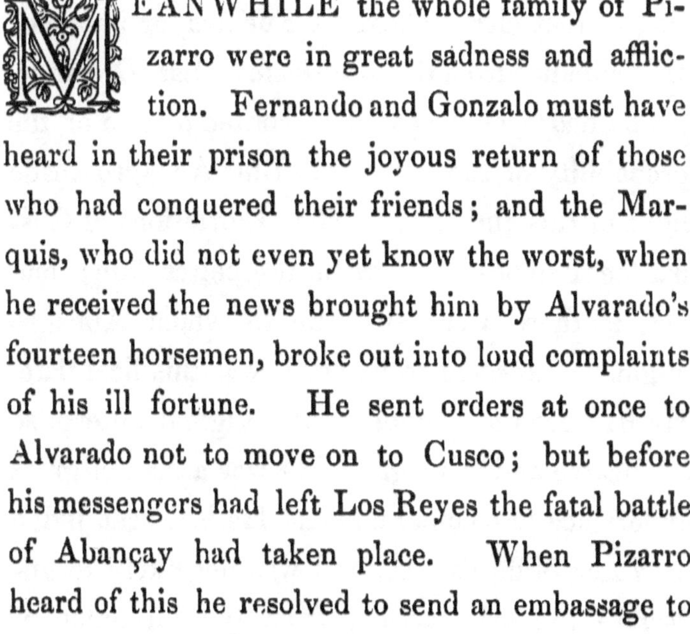

MEANWHILE the whole family of Pizarro were in great sadness and affliction. Fernando and Gonzalo must have heard in their prison the joyous return of those who had conquered their friends; and the Marquis, who did not even yet know the worst, when he received the news brought him by Alvarado's fourteen horsemen, broke out into loud complaints of his ill fortune. He sent orders at once to Alvarado not to move on to Cusco; but before his messengers had left Los Reyes the fatal battle of Abançay had taken place. When Pizarro heard of this he resolved to send an embassage to treat with Almagro. The persons he chose were the factor Illan Suarez de Carvajal, the licentiate Gaspar de Espinosa, Diego de Fuenmayor, a brother of the president of the *Audiencia* at San Domingo, and the licentiate de la Gama.

When these important personages had arrived at Cusco they found that they could make no way in their mission. Almagro said that he would not give up a hand's-breadth of the land which his Majesty had conferred upon him, and that he was determined to go to Los Reyes and take possession of that city. Diego de Fuenmayor produced an ordinance from the *Audiencia* of San Domingo, which had been prepared in contemplation of the probability of these feuds. But Almagro made light of this authority. The exhortations of Gaspar de Espinosa met with no better fate; and yet, if there were any one to whom Almagro might be expected to listen, it was this licentiate. He had been a partner in the original enterprise of Pizarro and Almagro. He was a man of great experience in colonial affairs. He had been judge in Vasco Nuñez's case, and was not likely to underrate the evils arising from the infraction of authority. " Are not, in truth," he said, " these regions wide enough to extend your authority in, without, for the sake of a few leagues more or less, doing that which will irritate Heaven, offend the King, and fill the world with scandals and disasters?"

But Almagro held firm to his resolve of maintaining what he considered to be his rights: whereupon Espinosa exclaimed, "Well, then, Señor Adelantado, that will come to pass here which the old Castilian proverb speaks of, ' The conquered conquered, and the conqueror ruined.'"*

Espinosa fell ill and died at Cusco; and the embassage proved entirely abortive. There is this to be said in defence of Almagro's conduct, that it was impossible for him now to do anything which was not full of danger and difficulty. Finally, he resolved to move forwards to Los Reyes, carrying Fernando Pizarro with him, and leaving Gonzalo Pizarro and Alonzo de Alvarado at Cusco, in the charge of a numerous body of guards. When Almagro halted in the valley of Lanasca, news reached him that Gonzalo Pizarro and the other prisoners had bribed their guards

---

* " El vencido vencido, y el Vencedor perdido."

and had escaped. Never was the life of Fernando Pizarro in greater danger. At Chincha Almagro again halted, and founded a new town, which was called after his own name.

Meanwhile, a favourable turn had taken place in the fortunes of the Marquis Pizarro, who was at Los Reyes. Auxiliaries had now come to him from the different quarters to which he had appealed for assistance.

Almagro, having been informed of the nature and number of Pizarro's forces, abandoned at once his plan of advancing to Los Reyes.

Pizarro's moderation and prudence were not abated by his growing strength in men and arms. (Men rather *became* his enemies than *were made* so). In obscurity at Panamá, and now in power at Los Reyes, he is always patient, much enduring, and what is often termed weak. He now resisted the vehement counsels of those captains who were smarting from their recent defeat at the bridge of Abançay; and sought to bring the question between himself and Almagro to an end by means of arbitration. Almagro now was in a humble mood; and so it was agreed that the Provincial Bobadilla, of the Order of Mercy, should be appointed judge of the case; who, with the assistance of " pilots," should fix the limits of the respective governments of New Castille and New Toledo.

Bobadilla took up his station at an Indian town named Mala, midway on the high road between Los Reyes and Chincha.

Thither he summoned both governors to appear before him, each to be attended by twelve horsemen only.

After the Marquis had set out, Gonzalo was induced by Pizarro's followers to advance with the army in the direction of Mala; as it was thought that Almagro's former treachery had put him beyond the pale of confidence.

When, however, the old companions, Pizarro and Almagro, met, it was with such tears and loving words as if nothing hitherto had happened to disturb their amity; and there was every prospect of their coming to terms before the sentence of arbitration should be pronounced. The moving up, however, of Gonzalo with Pizarro's army aroused the suspicions of Almagro's troops; one of the captains brought a horse to the door where the Governors were conferring, and contrived to give notice to Almagro of the supposed stratagem; upon which the Mariscal went down stairs without taking leave, got upon his horse, and went off with his friends at full gallop.

The Marquis sent the next day to tell Almagro that his army had moved without his leave; but it was of no avail. The arbiter, however, ordered certain persons who had been appointed by Almagro to appear before him; and he gave sentence entirely in Pizarro's favour, declaring that Cusco was within the two hundred and seventy-five leagues which the Emperor had assigned as the extent of Pizarro's government, and that the Mariscal should quit that territory, and go to the land of his own government.

When this sentence was communicated to the Mariscal, he declared he would not abide by it; and his men held that it was a most unrighteous judgment. It was, however, so much for the interest of both parties that some amicable conclusion should be arrived at, that negotiations were again commenced. Finally, a treaty was concluded that Fernando Pizarro should be liberated, Chincha evacuated; that Cusco should be put in deposit until the king should decide; that Almagro and his people should conquer the country in one direction, Pizarro and his in the other; lastly, that Pizarro should give Almagro a ship, which should be allowed to enter the port of Zangala or Chincha, wherever the vessel might happen to touch.

Orgoñez was furious at this treaty being concluded; and many of the soldiers fully agreed with him in the danger of setting Fernando Pizarro free. But Almagro and the friends of peace were not to be deterred from their resolve. Accordingly, the Mariscal, proceeding to the place of Fernando Pizarro's confinement, ordered him to be released. Immediately they embraced, and Fernando Pizarro took a solemn oath, pledging himself to fulfil what had been agreed upon. The Mariscal then carried him to his house and regaled him splendidly. All the chief men in the army visited him. Afterwards they accompanied him about half a league from the camp, and then took leave of him.

Almagro sent his son, Don Diego de Almagro, commonly called *el moço*,—"the youth,"—in company with Fernando Pizarro to the Marquis. Many cavaliers also went with them. The Marquis lavished courtesies and gifts upon them, and paid particular attention to Almagro's son. When these had returned to the camp, Almagro evacuated Chincha, and marched to the valley of Zangala, where he began to found another town.

At this time, the very day when Fernando Pizarro had been set at liberty, there suddenly arrived a messenger from the Court of Spain. His dispatches were that each of the Governors should retain whatever they had conquered and peopled, until any other arrangement should be made by his Majesty.

This royal order was in the highest degree satisfactory to the Pizarros, as it seemed to settle the question in the Marquis's favour with regard to the occupation of Cusco. Fernando Pizarro sought leave at this time to return to Spain and give an account to the Emperor of what had taken place in Peru; but his brother would not consent, saying that the Emperor would be better served by Fernando's staying to help him, the Marquis, to maintain his government.

Meanwhile, the Mariscal had, according to agreement, retired from Chincha, and the Marquis went there to seek provisions and to recommence the arrangements with Almagro, which would be necessary in consequence of the new ordinance from the Court of Spain. On the road to Chincha the Marquis's troops found the wells filled up, which they attributed to the Mariscal's men. When Pizarro had arrived at Chincha, he sent to Almagro to notify the royal orders to him, to which the Mariscal replied that these orders were in his favour, for, from where he was to Chincha, he had conquered and peopled the country, and, accordingly, he it was who was within the limits of his own government, and he begged that Pizarro would move out of it.

There is no doubt that both sides now believed themselves to be wronged and affronted. Orgoñez and his party, no doubt, clamoured loudly about the perfidy of the Pizarros. No sooner had a treaty been settled than these Pizarros hastened to recommence hostilities. This came of injudicious clemency.

On the other side, the conduct of the Almagristas was stigmatized by Pizarro's partisans in the harshest terms. The word they used was "tyranny," taken in the old Greek sense of the unlawful seizure of sovereignty; and to punish such tyranny, the whole of Pizarro's army moved forwards. The Mariscal, being made aware of this by his spies, withdrew to Guaytára, a pass in the sierra, so difficult, that to surmount it was considered equivalent to passing a great river three times. Pizarro's troops followed the Almagristas; but the latter looked upon their position as impregnable.

Fernando Pizarro, however (probably the greatest captain of his time in this kind of warfare), looked nly to where the difficulty was greatest, and where, therefore, the care of the enemy would be least; and this was where the body of Spanish troops was posted on the height. Early one evening Fernando Pizarro, taking with him three hundred of his most active men, made for this part of the sierra. At the foot of it they dismounted, and they had now a league of mountain to ascend —all of it sheer ascent. Moreover, Almagro's captain was informed of their enterprise (the Almagristas were much better served by spies than the other party); and he and his men waited for Fernando Pizarro, considering him to be a lost man. The Marquis stayed at the foot of the sierra, intending to follow if Fernando Pizarro should gain the pass. And the pass was gained. With darkness alone to aid them, heavily encumbered with arms and armour, being obliged sometimes to climb the more precipitous parts on their hands and knees, the Indians hurling down great stones upon them, sometimes sinking in the sand in such a way that instead of moving forwards they slid down again, they still contrived to reach the summit. It was an arduous task for Fernando Pizarro, a heavy man with ponderous armour, totally unaccustomed to go on foot; but his exertions were so strenuous as to astonish all beholders. It happened that five or six of Pizarro's soldiers gained the height at the same moment. They shouted " Viva el Rey !" with such vigour that the enemy, supposing the whole of the army was upon them, were panic-stricken, and fled at once. To show the difficult nature of this pass, it may be mentioned that it was midday before the whole three hundred reached the summit. Fernando Pizarro was greatly delighted with the success of his enterprise, and held it to be a happy omen for the future. The Marquis, with the rest of the troops, were now able at their ease to sur-

mount the pass.   Almagro and his troops retreated, and Pizarro's forces moved onwards in an
irregular and disjointed manner, being informed
that Almagro was making his way to Cusco.
After a few days' march, they arrived at the
highest point of a barren waste, where it rained and
snowed much, and the forces were so scattered
that on that night they had only two hundred
men together.

Now it happened that on that very night the
Almagristas were much nearer to Pizarro's men
than these imagined.   Indeed, Almagro's camp
was not more than a league off, and he was very
much bent upon making an attack upon Pizarro's
forces.   His reason for this was that a large part
of the Marquis's men were new comers, and it
was well known that in the snowy wastes of
Peru all strangers were apt to suffer from snow-
sickness, experiencing the same sensations as if
they were at sea;* but Orgoñez, for once in his
life cautious, and (as mostly happens when a man
acts or advises against the bent of his own disposition) acting wrongly, dissuaded Almagro from

* "Se marean como en un golfo de mar."

an enterprise which would probably have been fatal to the enemy.

As day broke, Pizarro's army saw the situation in which they were, and Fernando Pizarro, whose valour never left his wisdom far behind, counselled instant retreat. Their march had hitherto been but a disorderly pursuit, whereas the enemy's forces were in a state of good preparation for immediate action. The Marquis listened to his brother's advice, and the army retreated to the valley of Ica to recruit themselves. Then the principal captains besought Pizarro to return to Los Reyes, as, on account of his age, they said, he was unfit to endure the labours of such a campaign. The Governor consented; and, leaving Fernando Pizarro as his representative, returned to Los Reyes.

CHAPTER VI.

Fernando Pizarro marches to Cusco—The Battle of Salinas —The Execution of the Mariscal Almagro—Return of Fernando Pizarro to Spain.

ERNANDO PIZARRO, now placed in full command, resolved that with those who would follow him, whether they were many or whether they were few, he would go and take possession of that city of Cusco which he had lost.   Marching to the valley of Lanasca, he halted there and reviewed his men.

Almagro, on the other hand retired to Cusco, where he made the most vigorous preparations to withstand the coming attack of Fernando Pizarro. In Cusco nothing was heard but the sound of trumpets summoning to reviews, and the hammering of silver on the anvil, for of that metal it was that they made their corselets, morions, and arm-pieces, which they rendered, by using double the quantity of silver that they would have of iron, as strong "as if they had come from Milan." They resolved to await the attack of Fernando Pizarro within the city, fortifying it towards that part of the river where the defences were weak.

Meanwhile Fernando Pizarro was advancing slowly to Cusco, being so watchful that his men marched in their armour. Having arrived at a place called Acha, he rested there five days, for his men to recover from their fatigue. After-wards, he proceeded to a spot where there were three roads, and, to deceive the enemy's scouts, he proceeded to pitch his camp there. Then, when information had been carried to Orgoñez, who hastened to occupy a certain pass, Fernando Pizarro ordered the tents to be struck, marched the whole night, and occupied the pass at which the enemy had thought to stop him. Almagro's captains now changed their plan of remaining in the city. All that day Fernando Pizarro expected to meet his enemies in a great plain, which there is three leagues from Cusco, and, as he did not find them, he left the royal road with the intent of placing himself on an elevated spot in those plains, which are called the Salt Pits (Salinas).

Orgoñez now moved his own camp to a spot three quarters of a league from the city, between a sierra and a river. He himself occupied the plain with all his cavalry, who wore white vests over their armour.

Fernando Pizarro also made his preparation for battle. Over his armour he put on a surcoat or vest (*ropeta*) of orange damask, and in his morion a tall white feather, which floated over the heads of all. He did this, not only that he might be known by his own men, but by those of the opposite side, to whom, it is said, he sent notice of his dress. He had received indignities when in prison, and was anxious to meet his personal enemies in the field. He now first sent forward a notary to make a formal requisition that the city of Cusco should be delivered up to him; then he approached the spot where the enemy had pitched their camp.

We should judge but poorly of these combats in Spanish America, if we estimated them according to the smallness of the number of men engaged on each side, and not according to the depth and amount of human emotion which they elicited. There was more passion in the two little armies now set over against each other than is to be found in vast hosts of hireling soldiers combating for objects which they scarcely understand. I have no doubt the hatred in these bands of Almagristas and Pizarristas greatly exceeded anything that was to be found in the ranks of the French and Spaniards that fought at Pavia.

No answer was vouchsafed by Orgoñez to the formal demand made by Pizarro's notary for the cession of Cusco; and the battle commenced by Almagro's artillery beginning to play upon the advancing Pizarristas. At the first discharge it took off two of Fernando Pizarro's foot-soldiers, but the whole body of the infantry pressed on. Orgoñez drew his men back behind a little hill, not from a motive of fear, but with the design of letting some of the troops on the other side pass the river. Almagro, who was too ill to enter into the battle himself, but was watching it from a distance in a litter, construed this movement most unfavourably for his own fortunes. Descending from his litter he got on horseback, and rode off to Cusco, where he retreated into the fortress.

The cavalry on both sides were soon mingled in a hand-to-hand encounter; and Fernando Pizarro, well known to his enemies, was conspicuous in the *mêlée*. Pedro de Lerma, with all the fury of a traitor and a renegade, was the first to make his way where that white plume towered above the rest, and to bear down upon its owner. His lance, however, only struck Pizarro's horse in the neck, and drove it down upon its knees, but the more skilful Fernando pierced his adversary with his lance. Pedro de Lerma was, however, but one of many who had resolved on that day to chastise the insolence, as they would have said, of Fernando Pizarro. Though dismounted, Fernando was not injured, and drawing his sword he fought with his usual valour.

In the meantime the movement of Orgoñez's cavalry had laid open his infantry to a charge from the infantry of the Pizarristas under Gonzalo Pizarro, which proved most effective; and this charge was the turning point of the engagement. They fairly turned and fled up the sierra, eagerly pursued by Gonzalo, who feared lest the fugitives should make themselves strong in Cusco.

Most of the worsted cavaliers were taken prisoners, being protected by persons who knew them, and were brought before Fernando Pizarro, who, not listening to private vengeance, in his clemency spared them all.

Orgoñez lay dead upon the field. Fernando Pizarro sent Alonzo de Alvarado to take the Mariscal prisoner. He was conducted to the same apartment in which he had formerly confined Fernando Pizarro, and a promise was given him that he should be kindly treated and justice well considered in his case. Access to him was not denied, until it was found that he was endeavouring to gain over Pizarro's captains. A formal process was instituted against him, which took nearly four months in its preparation.

This battle of Salinas was fought on the 6th of April, 1538, five years and a-half after Francisco Pizarro had first marched to meet Atahuallpa at Cassamarca.

Fernando Pizarro went to the extreme of graciousness in his conduct to the vanquished. He employed a number of Almagro's soldiers, and sent them on different expeditions. The commander of one of these, Pedro de Candia, was won over by some of these soldiers to contemplate returning to Cusco to release Almagro.

Within the city, too, there was treachery. Fernando Pizarro learned that there were two hundred persons banded together to release the imprisoned Mariscal; and, moreover, these had posted friends of theirs at difficult passes on the road to Los Reyes, in order that they might set Almagro at liberty, if Fernando Pizarro should send him to Spain, there to be judged by the Emperor.   Then there came a letter from a man named Villacastin, an alcalde of Cusco, who had gone out to visit the Indians, which had been given in *encomienda* to him.   This man had met with Pedro de Candia's people, had been ill-treated by them, and had heard of their intention to resist Gonzalo Pizarro, who had been sent out to compel them to proceed on their expedition.

Pizarro now summoned a council of the regidors, alcaldes, and some of the captains of best repute for judgment, and who appeared to him most dispassionate, and begged them to counsel him, as men of honour and good judgment, what ought to be done, that his Majesty might be served and the city maintained in peace; and lest any of them should not give their opinions in his presence with perfect freedom, he would prefer to go out of the council; but what they should advise he would carry out. The council came to the decision that, deserving death as Almagro did, the lesser evil would be to pass sentence upon him and to execute the sentence, since, if this were not done, a great mischief was impending over them. Great was the anguish of the old decrepit Mariscal upon the sentence of death being notified to him. He at once appealed from Fernando Pizarro to the Emperor, but Fernando would not allow this appeal to be received. He then besought him, in the most piteous manner, to spare his life, urging, as a plea for mercy, the great part he had taken in the early fortunes of Fernando's brother, the Marquis, reminding him also of his own (Fernando's) release, and that no blood of the Pizarro family had been shed by him. Lastly, he bade him consider how old, weak, and infirm he was, and begged that he would allow the appeal to go on to the Emperor, so that he might spend in prison the few and sorrowful days which remained for him, to mourn over his sins. This Fernando Pizarro refused. He said that, though Almagro's crimes had been very great, he would not have sentenced him, but would have sent him to the Emperor, had not the conspiracies of his partisans been such as to prevent that course. Then he told him that he wondered that a man of such valour should show this fear of death. To which the other replied, that since our Lord Jesus Christ feared death, it was not much that he, a man and a sinner, should fear it. But Fernando Pizarro would not recede from his purpose, though, it is said, he felt the greatest pity for Almagro. Pizarro having quitted the apartment, Almagro made his confession; and being counselled, as his estate was forfeited for treason, to leave it by will to the Emperor, he did so. His worldly and his spiritual affairs being thus settled, he was strangled in prison, in order to avoid any outbreak which a public execution might have caused in Cusco. That there might be no doubt, however, of his death, the body was shown in the great square, with the head cut off. This was on the 8th of July, 1538.

Thus died Almagro, at the age of sixty-five

years. Like his partner, the Marquis, he was a natural son, brought up in ignorance,—for he could not read. He had all the gifts of a first-rate common soldier, but seems to have had no especial ability as a commander. Profusely and splendidly generous, he had the art of attaching men to him who were far greater than himself in most things; and these attachments did not die out at his death. As men are seldom really attracted to other men but by some great quality, Almagro's generosity must have been of that deep nature which goes far beyond gifts, and where the recipient perceives that his benefactor loves as well as benefits him. In watching the career of Almagro, it is necessary to account in some such way for the singular affection which he uniformly inspired.

As for Fernando Pizarro, it is most probable that, in this matter, which has darkened his name with posterity, he had no other intention at first but that of sending Almagro to Spain for judgment. But the unwise endeavours of Almagro's own people made it seem a duty to the stern Fernando to put the Mariscal to death; and Fernando Pizarro was a man of that mould, upon which the speeches of other men, past, present, and to come, would have but little influence. He probably foresaw that he would be severely condemned for this transaction, and, far from being deterred on that account, would resolutely beware of giving way to any feeling for his own reputation, which might be detrimental to the public service. His conduct, however, on this occasion, is one of those things which can never be made clear, and where a man, let him have acted from what good motive he may, must go down to posterity with a grievous stain upon his reputation.

This execution, like most cruelties, did not ensure the desired object: it did not prove final; but, on the contrary, formed a fresh starting-point for calamities of still deeper dye.

As on Atahuallpa's death, so on that of the Mariscal, the funeral rites due to his dignity were not forgotten. Pizarro's captains were the supporters of Almagro's bier. He was interred very honourably in the church of " Our Lady of Mercy; " and the brothers Fernando and Gonzalo Pizarro put on mourning in honour of the Mariscal of Peru.

As if to show how little the shedding of blood avails, the funeral rites were no sooner ended than the King's officers who had served under Almagro, namely, the Treasurer, the Contador, and the Veedor, made a formal intimation to Fernando Pizarro that the government now belonged to them, and they required him to quit that country. To this audacious requisition, which was merely reopening a question which had been settled as Fernando Pizarro thought, he replied by seizing upon their persons, and then went out immediately to quell the mutineers under Pedro de Candia. For this purpose he took with him eighty horsemen. Many of the mutineers, when they heard the news of Almagro's death, and of Fernando's approach, fled; and the captains came out of the camp to receive Fernando Pizarro. With his usual dignified bravery, when he was within half a league of them, he left his guard behind, and approached the opposite party, attended only by an alguazil and a notary. He then took the necessary informations, and, ascertaining that a captain of his own, named De Mesa, had been the ringleader of the revolt, he caused him to be immediately executed, while he sent Pedro de Candia, with some others of the principal captains, to the Marquis, his brother.

On that same day, Fernando Pizarro busied himself in giving liberty to many Indian men and women, whom Pedro de Candia's people had brought as prisoners in chains; and he also provided for their return to their own lands, for which the poor Indians were very grateful, giving thanks to their gods, and praising Fernando Pizarro. He appointed Pedro de Ançurez as captain in Pedro de Candia's room; and, still fearing for the welfare of the Indians, Fernando himself accompanied the expedition. "For," as it is said, " as he went with them, they did not dare to do any mischief to the peaceable natives, nor to seize them, nor to put them in bonds." It is impossible not to give Fernando Pizarro credit for a stern sense of duty, when we find him ready to offend friends and enemies alike, by acts which could only have been dictated by natural goodness of heart, or by his regard for the orders he had received from the home government, on behalf of the Indians, when he was in Spain.

Fernando Pizarro had sent the young Almagro, commonly called " *Almagro el moço*," to the Marquis, who did not fail to give the young man comforting assurances respecting his father's life. After a time, the Marquis, thinking that it would be necessary for him to set affairs in order at Cusco, as Fernando Pizarro was going to Spain, proceeded from Los Reyes to that city. It was not until he reached the bridge of Abançay that he heard of the condemnation and execution of Almagro. Casting down his eyes, he remained for a long time looking on the ground, and weeping. There have been writers who supposed that the Marquis had sanctioned Almagro's death; but there is no ground whatever for such a supposition, and there is no doubt that the tears shed by him for his old comrade were tears of genuine sorrow. Had he left Los Reyes earlier, the mischief would have been averted. When he reached Cusco, the Marquis found both his brothers absent, as they were engaged in an important expedition amongst the Indians in the vicinity of the great lake of Titicaca. After his return from this enterprise, Fernando Pizarro quitted Peru for Spain, in order to give his Majesty an account of what had taken place; but several friends of Almagro, amongst them Diego de Alvarado, to whom Almagro had committed the execution of his last wishes, had reached Spain before Fernando Pizarro. A suit was instituted against Fernando; and Diego de Alvarado challenged him to mortal combat, which was prevented by the sudden death of the challenger. Fernando Pizarro, however, was not freed from the suit. One of the principal charges against him was his having given liberty to Manco Inca, which was alleged to have been the cause of the Indian revolt. In this matter, however, he was only so far to blame that he had been indulgent to the Inca, and had permitted him to go out of the city of Cusco to make certain sacrifices to his father. For the death of Almagro, which was the next great charge against Fernando Pizarro, his motives have been already given. Fernando Pizarro failed, however, to exculpate himself; and, being deprived of the habit of Santiago, he was detained in prison at Medina del Campo for twenty-three years. Being at last freed, he retired to his estate in the country, where he died, having attained the great age of one hundred years. It was a melancholy ending for so renowned a man, and one who, to the best of his ability and understanding, had laboured largely for the Crown.   Still, it must be admitted that the events which followed in Peru formed a standing condemnation of the harshness of his conduct in prohibiting the appeal of Almagro to the Emperor, a harshness which in his long years of durance (how wearisome to so impatient a spirit!) he must have had ample time to understand and to regret.

CHAPTER VII.

The Marquis and the Men of Chili — Gonzalo Pizarro discovers the Amazon — The Conspiracy of Almagro's Friends—The Marquis Pizarro is murdered by the Men of Chili.

THE Marquis now remained the sole posessor of supreme authority throughout the empire of Peru. His brother Fernando, fearing lest Almagro's son should prove a centre of faction, had, before his departure, urged the Marquis to send the young man to Spain; but Pizarro did not listen to this prudent advice. Neither was his treatment of the conquered party judicious in other respects. Not knowing the maxim of Machiavelli, that in such cases it is better to destroy than to impoverish, Pizarro left Almagro's men, the men of Chili, in poverty and idleness; but scorned to persecute them. Finding, however, that they resorted to the house of young Almagro, the Marquis was persuaded by his counsellors to deprive him of his Indians. The men of Chili fell into the most abject poverty, and there is a story that seven of them, who messed together, had only one cloak among them. And these were men who had been accustomed to command, who had known many vicissitudes of prosperity and adversity, and were not likely to accept any misfortune as if it were final. One attempt Pizarro made to aid and favour these dangerous persons, but his overtures were then coldly rejected by them. They were waiting, with a patient desire for vengeance, the arrival of a judge from Spain, named Vaca de Castro, from whom they expected the condemnation of those who had been concerned in the death of Almagro.

Meanwhile the Marquis pursued his course of conquering new territories and founding new cities. He despatched Pedro de Valdivia to Chili, and he, succeeding where Almagro failed, has always been considered the conqueror of that country. The Marquis sent his brother Gonzalo to the southern district of Collao, conquered that territory in which lay the mines of Potosi, and gave rich *repartimientos* to his brothers, Gonzalo and Martin, and their followers.

After all his conquests, it was but a strip of sea-board that Pizarro occupied and governed, when compared with the boundless regions of South America, even to this day but sparsely occupied or ruled over by civilized man. The Marquis, however, now originated an enterprise, which, leading men to the eastern side of the Andes, was to make them acquainted with regions of the New World far more extensive than had ever yet been discovered in any single enterprise by land. There was a region where cinnamon-trees were known to abound, and it was into this cinnamon country, neighbouring to Quito, that the Marquis sent his brother Gonzalo, at the end of the year 1539. In order to facilitate the enterprise, the Marquis bestowed on his brother the government of Quito. Gonzalo set out from Quito in January, 1540, with three hundred Spaniards and four thousand Indians. The sufferings the expedition went through, even from the commencement of the march, were intense.

Nevertheless, with the patience and perseverance of a Pizarro, Gonzalo toiled on, being always foremost in the work, whether it was cutting down timber, making charcoal, or labouring at the forge. At last they came to a large river; and there they resolved to build a brigantine, and launch it upon the waters. They now thought their labours were over: Gonzalo manned the brigantine with fifty soldiers, placing at their head a captain of good repute, Francisco de Orellana. They had learned from some Indians that, ten days' journey down, this river joined another large river. The brigantine was to go down to this point, leave there the sick and the baggage, and return with provisions for the main body of the expedition. The voyage was commenced, but Orellana never returned to them. He stole off with the brigantine and, proceeding down the river, was the first to traverse that vast continent. At the end of his voyage of two thousand five hundred miles, he found himself in the Atlantic, nearly at the same degree of latitude at which he had started.

Meanwhile Gonzalo, finding Orellana did not return, constructed some canoes and rafts, and journeying partly by land, and partly by water, contrived in two months to reach the junction of the rivers, where he learned the treachery of Orellana from a Spaniard he had put ashore there. This great river, now known by the name of the Amazon, was then called, after its discoverer, the Orellana.   The honour and fame of the discovery belongs really to the Pizarros, to the Marquis, — the old discoverer of Peru, who had pondered so long upon what Comogre's son had to tell of the riches of the south,— for originating the enterprise, and to Gonzalo next, by whose much-enduring perseverance the expedition was led on, through so much difficulty, to its banks.

But, while Gonzalo was in these straits, robbed by Orellana of fame, and left almost to perish from want, his brother and chief was in still greater peril at Los Reyes. His untiring enemies, the men of Chili, were all this time unsoothed and discontented, and therefore dangerous. The head of the defeated faction was a resolute and clever soldier, Juan de Rada, who had been major-domo in the household of the Mariscal. This man took the young Almagro, a youth of eighteen or nineteen, under his guardianship, and entirely managed the affairs of the men of Chili.

They were now doubly disappointed and dis contented, because they had found that the judge whom they were expecting from Spain, to avenge the death of Almagro and to do justice to his cause, was not entrusted with powers to con- demn, but only with a commission to inquire, and to transmit the result of his inquiries to Spain. They had hoped to find an avenger in him.

The men of Chili were no longer few in number. There had gradually come into Los Reyes about two hundred of them,—needy, disfavoured, dis- contented men. Insults began to be interchanged between the rival factions, — insults, as mostly happened in these colonies, of a grotesque and dramatic nature. One day, early in the morning, the populace of Los Reyes were amused by seeing three ropes suspended in the public pillory in the great square. The upper end of one rope was so placed as to point to the Marquis's palace, while the house of his secretary, Juan Picado, and that of his alcalde mayor, Doctor Velazquez, were pointed at in a similar manner by the ends of the other two ropes. The Marquis's friends saw in this insult the handiwork of the men of Chili, and begged the Marquis to punish them. The good-natured Pizarro said that they already were sufficiently punished in being poor, and conquered, and ridden over. The Spanish blood of his followers, however, could not brook the insult they had received, or desist from attempting to reply to it. Accordingly, the populace of Los Reyes were again amused by seeing Antonio Picado ride through the street where the young Almagro lived, wearing a cap adorned with a gold medal that had a silver fig embossed upon it, and a motto in these words, " For the men of Chili." Great was the wrath of the followers of Almagro at this absurd insult.

The rumour that the men of Chili meditated something desperate was rife even among the Indians, and the Marquis's friends warned him of his danger. Besides, it was noticed that Juan de Rada was buying a coat of mail. On the other hand, it was observed by the men of Chili that Pizarro had been purchasing lances.

Juan de Rada was sent for by Pizarro. The Governor was in his garden, looking at some orange-trees, when the leader of the men of Chili called upon him. " What is this, Juan de Rada," said the Marquis, " that they tell me, of your buying arms to kill me?" " It is true, my lord, that I have bought two cuirasses and a coat of mail to defend myself." " Well," replied the Marquis, " but what moves you to buy armour now, more than at any other time?" " Because they tell us, and it is notorious, that your lordship is buying lances to slay us all. Let your lordship finish with us; for, having commenced by destroying the head, I do not know why you should have any respect for the feet. It is also said that your lordship intends to slay the judge who is coming from Spain; but, if your intention is such, and you are determined to put to death the party of Almagro, at least spare Don Diego, for he is innocent. Banish him, and I will go with him wherever fortune may please to carry us."

The Marquis was enraged at these words. " Who has made you believe such great villainy and treachery of me?" he exclaimed; " I never thought of such a thing, and I am more desirous than you that this judge should come, who already

would be here, if he had embarked in the galleon
I sent for him. As to the story of the spears, the
other day I went hunting, and amongst the whole
party there was not one who had a spear.   I
ordered my servants to buy one; and they have
bought four. Would to God, Juan de Rada,
the judge were here, so that these things might
have an end, and that God may make the truth
manifest!"

"By heaven, my lord!" replied Juan de Rada,
somewhat softened by the Governor's response,
"but they have made me get into debt for more
than five hundred *pesos,* which I have spent in
buying armour, and so I have a coat of mail to
defend myself against whoever may wish to slay
me." "Please God, Juan de Rada, I shall do
nothing of the kind," responded the Marquis.
The conference ended thus, and Juan de Rada
was going, when Pizarro's jester, who was standing by, said, "Why don't you give him some of
these oranges?"   As they were the first that
were grown in that country, they were much
esteemed. "You say well," replied the Marquis;
and he gathered six of them, and gave them to
Juan de Rada, adding that he should tell him if

he wanted anything. They then separated amicably, Juan de Rada kissing the Governor's hands as he took leave.

This interview reassured Pizarro, but did not divert the conspirators from their designs. Again and again Pizarro was warned. Twice he received intelligence from a certain clerigo in whom one of the conspirators had confided. Others gave the Marquis the same information, but he contented himself with giving orders, in a lukewarm manner, to his alcalde mayor to arrest the principal men of Chili. This officer replied, that his lordship need have no fear as long as he held the rod of office in his hand.

The next day was Sunday, June 26, 1541. Pizarro did not go to mass, probably from some fear of being attacked. When mass was ended the principal inhabitants called upon the Marquis; but, after paying their respects, went away, leaving him with his brother Martin, his alcalde mayor, and Francisco de Chaves, an intimate friend.

Meanwhile the conspirators were collected together in the house of Don Diego Almagro. Nothing was resolved upon as to the day on which they were to make the attack, and Juan de Rada was sleeping, when a certain Pedro de San Millan entered, and exclaimed, " What are you about? In two hours' time they are coming to cut us to pieces, for so the treasurer Riquelme has just said." This was probably a version of the fact that Pizarro had ordered the arrest of the principal conspirators.

There is a strong family-likeness in conspiracies. For a time there is much indecision, until some imminent peril to the conspirators hastens the result, and determines the hour of the deed. Juan de Rada sprang from his bed, armed himself, and addressed a short speech to his followers, urging them to avenge the death of Almagro, to aspire to dominion in Peru, and, if these motives weighed not with them, at least to strike a blow in order to protect themselves against a pressing danger. This speech was received with acclamations, and immediate action was resolved upon. The first thing the conspirators did was to hang out a white flag from the window, as a signal to their accomplices that they must arm and come to their assistance. They then sallied forth. It is probable, as it was mid-day, that there were not many persons in the streets or in the great square.

The conspirators shouted " Down with the tyrant traitor who has caused the judge to be killed whom the King has sent." The few persons who noticed the march of this furious band merely observed to one another, " They are going to kill Picado or the Marquis." As they entered the great square, one of them, named Gomez Perez, made a slight detour, in order to avoid a little pool of water, which by chance had been spilt there from some conduit. Juan de Rada splashed through the pool, went straight to the dainty person, and said to him, " We are going to bathe ourselves in human blood, and you hesitate to dip your feet in water. You are not a man for this business: go back." Nor did he suffer him to proceed further.

The conspirators gained the house of Pizarro without opposition. It was strong, having two courts and a great gate. The Marquis was not entirely surprised. His brother Martin, the alcalde Doctor Velazquez, and Francisco de Chaves, had dined with him. The dinner was just over, when some of his Indians rushed in to give him notice of the approach of the men of Chili. He ordered Francisco de Chaves to shut to the door of the hall, and of the apartment in which they were. That officer, supposing that it was some riot among the soldiers, which his authority would quell, went out to meet them, and found the conspirators coming up the staircase. They fell upon him at once, slew him, and threw the body down the stairs. Those who were in the dining hall, chiefly servants, rushed out to ascertain what was the matter; but, seeing Francisco de Chaves lying dead, fled back, and threw themselves out of the window, which opened upon the garden. Amongst them was Doctor Velazquez, who, as he leaped from the window, held his wand of office in his mouth; so that it was afterwards jestingly said, that he was right in telling his master the Marquis that he was safe as long as he, Doctor Velazquez, held the rod of office in his hands.

The conspirators pressed through the hall to the room where the Marquis himself was. He had found time to throw off his purple robe, to put on a cuirass, and to seize a spear. In this extremity there were by his side his half-brother, Francis Martin de Alcantara, a gentleman named Don Gomez de Luna (not hitherto mentioned), and

two pages.   Pizarro was then about seventy
years old.   He had commanded small companies
of Spaniards, making head on the field against
innumerable Indians, and had felt no doubt about
the result.   But now, with two men and two
lads, he had to contend for his life against nineteen practised soldiers.   The heroic courage of
the Marquis did not desert him at this last
moment.   He fought valiantly, while he de-
nounced, in the boldest words, the treachery and
the villainy of his assailants.   They only exclaimed:—" Kill him ! kill him ! let us not waste
our time."   Thus the mortal contest raged for a
short period.   At length Juan de Rada thrust one
of his companions forward upon Pizarro's spear,
and gained an entrance into the room.   The combat was now soon closed.   Martin de Alcantara,
Don Gomez de Luna, and the two pages, fell
slain by the side of Pizarro, who still continued to
defend himself.   At last, a wound in the throat
brought him to the ground.   While lying there,
he made the sign of a cross upon the ground, and
kissed it.   He was still alive, and was asking for
a confessor, when some base fellow dashed a jug
upon his prostrate face ; and, on receiving that

contemptible blow, the patient endurer of wearisome calamities, the resolute discoverer of long-
hidden lands, the stern conqueror of a powerful
nation, breathed his last.

THE END.

CHISWICK PRESS:—PRINTED BY WHITTINGHAM AND WILKINS,
TOOKS COURT, CHANCERY LANE.

9 783337 383213